# THE THREE HARES
# HARES

## THE JADE DRAGONBALL

# THE THREE HARES

## THE JADE DRAGONBALL

### SCOTT LAUDER
### AND DAVID ROSS

NEEM TREE
PRESS

Published by Neem Tree Press Limited 2019

Neem Tree Press Limited, 1st Floor,
2 Woodberry Grove, London, N12 0DR, UK
info@neemtreepress.com

Copyright © Scott Lauder and David Ross, 2019

A catalogue record for this book is available from the British Library

ISBN 978-1-911107-17-0 Paperback
ISBN 978-1-911107-04-0 Ebook

Printed and bound in Great Britain
by Biddles Limited

# CONTENTS

# PART 1

# BEIJING, CHINA
## THE PRESENT DAY

# CHAPTER 1

—

'Good morning!'

Sara recoiled from the cheery brightness of her parents' voices. She didn't do bright and cheery, not first thing in the morning. Flopping onto the hard kitchen bench, she scrunched her eyes against the sunlight glaring off the white walls, counters and appliances. It was just too much.

'Morning,' she yawned, resting her head on her hands.

Her father glanced up from *The Southern Daily* in his hands.

'Didn't sleep well,' Sara mumbled.

'Why…?' her father began, but Sara's mother set a plate down between them.

'Well, there's lots to do today. I do hope you weren't reading late, Sara.' Her mother continued: 'When you come back this afternoon, you'll need to finish your packing and say goodbye to Granny Tang.'

Sara grunted, irritated. Her packing was already finished! She stared at the slice of bread on her plate. She really wasn't hungry, but then again, she didn't want her stomach to rumble like yesterday morning in the Physics class. It had sounded like a Beijing subway train rolling through the school. She dug her knife into the extra-crunchy peanut butter and spread it absentmindedly on the slice.

Her father was again engrossed in his morning paper. A headline caught Sara's eye. She couldn't see all of it because of the folds in the newspaper, but what she could see read: '*Three … hares … all*'. Below the headline, the folds showed a strange, distorted picture: a head with two large ears sticking out of it. She brought the peanut-buttered bread to her lips... and froze. Her eyes locked onto a black and white photograph on the lower right of the paper: a thin-faced man and the words 'Bai Lu'.

Everything around her disappeared instantly, leaving her in complete darkness. A bitter, oppressive cold gnawed deep into her body. Was it a cave? An alley? It was impossible to know for sure in the pitch-blackness. She could sense walls surrounding her. The space felt tight, like a prison cell. She extended her right arm very, very slowly. At full extension, her hand bumped against icy stone. Her fingers slid warily along the stone, tracing the bumps and grooves and lines: a mouth with, it seemed, a tongue flopping out, teeth, a long snout, ears, a long scaly body. It was a dragon.

A stone dragon.

She dropped her hand and spun around. She heard breathing. Someone was in the space with her. She held her breath. Suddenly more terrified than she had ever been in her life, she punched her hands in front of her, twisting one way then the other. Nothing; then... She stumbled back, mouth open, the scream frozen in her mouth. In front of her, shimmering and floating in the gloom, something was writhing and groping towards her...

'No!' Sara cried. And as quickly as the vision appeared, it vanished. She was at the breakfast table again, looking across at her father's puzzled face.

'No... what?' he asked.

Sara's mother had paused squeezing the oranges to stare at her too.

'No... er. No school soon,' she said, trying to smile while her heart pounded madly.

Her father peered closely at her, frowning. He coughed and returned to his paper, rustling it noisily.

'Juice?' her mother asked, placing a glass of freshly squeezed orange juice on the table. Sara nodded. Her right hand was still trembling; the juice sloshed from side to side, almost spilling. She grasped it with both hands and took a gulp.

What had just happened? Had she just remembered part of a bad dream? Had she hallucinated? Had a mini stroke? Nothing – *nothing* like that had *ever* happened before. She'd been in a cave with a dragon on the wall – and what was that *thing* that had floated towards her?

She took another gulp just as her father changed position, revealing the whole of the newspaper's front page. Its main headline read: '*Three Arrested as Shares Fall*'. Below, there was a picture showing three men, hands in the air, being led away by police. The caption said the arrests were made at a company called Bai Lu because the three men had been…

Her father put down the paper. 'Suppose I better get going… Everything okay?' he looked straight at Sara.

Eyes down, Sara nodded.

'Okay, well, see you later,' he said. 'And what time do you finish tonight, dear?'

'I'll be back around nine,' her mother replied, returning his peck on the cheek.

'Holidays!' her father cried before he closed the front door of the apartment.

Sara's mother grinned. Sara tried to grin back, barely managing a half-smile. To calm herself down, she opened her favourite app – *Word of the Day* – on her phone and checked today's new word. She almost laughed when she saw it.

The word for today was 'grimace' – an ugly, twisted facial expression.

# CHAPTER 2

Still shaky from breakfast, Sara stepped out of her apartment block at the Palm Springs development into the early morning sunshine and heard them: cicadas. Not the peep-peeping of car horns. Not the shouts of pedestrians. Not the clatter of shop shutters. Not the low rumble of Beijing's 21 million inhabitants going about their lives.

Instead, it was the cicadas' loud, thrumming song that filled the humid morning air – and her head. They seemed even louder than normal. *Were they trying to break their own record for being the world's noisiest insect?* she wondered. Cicadas weren't exactly her favourite things – they had thick black bodies, bulging eyes and spooky, transparent wings – but they were incredible creatures. Some of them lived underground for 17 years, so when they finally saw the light of day, they were three years older than she was!

As she walked along the road, trying to forget about her odd experience over breakfast, she looked into the leaves and branches above her. There were many ash trees along this stretch of the route and she guessed there were hundreds of cicadas in each of them. Without stopping, she tried to spot one. She couldn't. Probably a good idea for them to stay hidden. Although some people liked them for their song, others thought they were tasty. In the Shandong region, where her mother was born, cicadas were deep-fried and eaten on sticks.

Cicadas also appeared in *The Thirty-Six Stratagems*, an ancient Chinese text her teacher, Mr Lee, had mentioned yesterday in their Chinese language and literature class. According to him, the ancients believed these ugly insects demonstrated something useful: how to fight against enemies with superior strength. Cicadas cast off their exoskeletons, and, similarly, people should also leave behind all that makes them recognisable in order to escape from harm. Having escaped, they rebuild their strength. Then, when they are ready, they return and confront the enemy.

Sara half-smiled. The thought of crushing her enemies sounded great... apart from the fact that she didn't have any. Of course, she didn't get along with everyone – there were a few people on the bus, for example, she disliked, and others in the school, too. But enemies? She wouldn't call them that.

Behind her, she heard the familiar growls of the school bus approaching. Skipping forward, she arrived at the stop just as the bus ground to a complete halt. Waiting for the doors to fold open, she glanced to her right and groaned. Out of a dirty window, two faces were staring at her. The Ferdinand brothers. As she watched them, they quickly pressed their lips against the window and breathed out, puffing up their cheeks and widening their eyes. *They're about as pretty as cicadas*, she thought, shaking her head. She had lost count of how many times they had done that. For them at least, the 'joke' never seemed to get old. The Ferdinand brothers were 14, too, but they acted as if they were six.

'All aboard!' the bus driver cried.

Sara hopped on. Ignoring the Ferdinand brothers, she waved to Lily and Joaquin, and made her way down the bus as it lurched forward. Sara sat with her friends and chatted for a while, but then the three of them fell silent. Today was the second to last day of school, and tomorrow was the trip to the Beijing Palace Museum. Not that anyone looked particularly excited about it.

In the seat in front of her, Joaquin was dozing – his head lolling side to side, the curls in his hair flopping this way and that. Next to her, Lily was listening to something – eyes closed, head back, ear buds in and glasses slightly askew. Sara leaned a little closer. Faintly, the crashing bass and drums of Deep Fried Lettuce, Lily's favourite band, leaked out. Sara smiled, then yawned. She was sleepy too. She leaned her head against Lily's shoulder and closed her eyes.

As soon as she did, she found herself standing at one end of a very wide, immeasurably long, mirrored walkway suspended in the sky. She gazed at the white, fluffy clouds and crystal blue sky reflected along the length of it. All the way at the other end was an enormous book whose pages were so huge that gales blew out at their every turn. She leaned into the ferocious blasts of air, bracing as the pages fell, until the book was suddenly still and, with letters written 15 metres high, revealed her name like a gigantic finger coming out of the clouds and pointing at her.

She blinked open her eyes. Lily was listening to Deep Fried Lettuce, Joaquin was practically snoring, and the bus was grinding towards the school. She frowned. Another very odd experience, but at least this one wasn't frightening, just very strange. Why was her imagination going into overdrive today? *The idea was probably in a book I read*, she thought. Books could do that – pull you in, really make you feel as though you were there. She was always getting carried away imagining things – additional scenes for books she had read, further adventures for their characters. But, as she stepped off the bus that bright morning, there was a tightness in her stomach, a vague but gnawing uneasiness.

Something didn't feel right.

# CHAPTER 3

—

'Psssst! Deadstone!' a voice behind her whispered.

Snorts and muffled laughter.

Sara kept staring straight ahead, her eyes firmly on Ms Ling who was standing at the front of the class, head down, trying to open a Powerpoint presentation for their class project, *The Art of Asia*. Didn't these name-callers ever get tired of their silly games?

'Hey, Rolling Stone!' A different voice this time, also behind her.

Obviously not. Such… what was the word? She pressed her lips together… Got it. Puerile – such puerile behaviour. She liked learning new words – they especially helped in her literature class, making the essays she wrote more expressive. It had been on her *Word of the Day* app a week or two ago. She smiled. Puerile meant childish; like a *boy*. How appropriate.

'Hey, Gallstone!'

More sniggers.

Sitting next to Sara, her friend Lily tut-tutted. Sara and Lily exchanged glances. They were thinking the exact same thing: *so* pathetic, *so* lame. Sara sighed. It was bad enough that Tony and Francis Ferdinand attended the same international school in Beijing as Sara. And it was bad enough that Tony and Francis were in the same class. But why, oh why, had Ms Ling put them in the seats behind her? Of all the people to choose from, why had she chosen them? The Ferdinand brothers were always doing this, always teasing her about her last name – Livingstone. Any moment now, they would say something.

'Sara Livingstun ah prezume!' And there it was, the fake Scottish accent. That came from Tony. His voice was slightly less annoying than his brother's whine, but only just. Yes, her father came from Scotland, and yes, her mother was Chinese. But so what? No one cared. Well, no one except the Ferdinand brothers.

The Gerbil – real name Lindsay but called The Gerbil because of her tawny hair, sunken eyes and plump cheeks – was sitting with her friend Jaz in front of Sara and Lily. Turning, she gave a sneering grin at the brothers' comments. Sara had no idea why The Gerbil disliked her. As far as Sara could remember, she had never done anything to her. According to Lily, Sara was smarter and that was enough. The words 'What's so funny?' hovered on the tip of Sara's tongue, desperate to escape. Instead, she clamped her jaws together and took a deep breath. Out of the corner of her eye, she noticed Joaquin frowning. Not surprising – he was her friend and the Ferdinand brothers weren't exactly his favourite people either. As Lily liked to say, they really were exemplary morons.

'What's the matter? Why aren't you talking to us?' This time it was Francis. His voice sounded like the noise someone makes when they hold their nose and try to speak at the same time. Sara had had enough. She opened her mouth, ready to tell them to shut up, but Lily got there first.

'Why don't you leave her alone and grow up?' Lily yelled, pushing her glasses back onto the bridge of her nose and giving the brothers her best death-laser stare.

Sara cringed. Heads turned.

'Lily Adorno! What *exactly* is the problem?'

Lily's head snapped to the front of the class.

'Well?' said Ms Ling, her brows gathering. 'What is it that you want to say?'

'S-Sorry, Ms Ling,' said Lily.

Ms Ling gave Lily her own death-laser stare, and time – for Sara, at least – seemed to slow down and stop.

The flashdrive went *bing*.

'Finally!' said Ms Ling, immediately losing interest in Lily and turning her attention to the presentation instead. She clicked on the first slide – the Qingming Scroll – and dimmed the lights. 'Tomorrow, as you know, we are going to visit the museum and see the Qingming Scroll, but before that, I would like to tell you a little bit about the history of this artwork and the Silk Road.'

And so the lecture began.

Art and history weren't really Sara's favourite subjects – she preferred English literature. But as Ms Ling told them all about the delicately painted silk scroll and how it showed everyday life in the Northern Song era, she forgot all about the Ferdinand brothers and focused on the artwork. It was a thousand years old, the work of the great painter Zhang Zeduan, and was about five metres long and just under the height of a 30cm ruler. There were hundreds of people in the painting – Ms Ling said over 800! Many were wearing simple clothes like breeches though others wore colourful gowns with long, draped sleeves. There was even someone on a donkey wearing a hat that looked like a sombrero! The scroll started in the countryside by a calm river and then became a road into a large town alongside a fast-moving river. There were so many boats lining the riverside. Most of the buildings were two stories high and had traditional sloped Chinese roofs, but at the left hand of the scroll there was a huge pagoda-shaped gateway with wide steps all the way to the top. There were restaurants with cafe seating outside, shops, people on wooden carts pulled by horses, bearers carrying sedan chairs. Her eyes darted from one corner of the scroll's landscape to the other. It was like nothing she had ever seen: the delicate colours, the incredible detail, the hustle and bustle, the feeling of everything being *alive*.

The next slide in the presentation was a close-up picture of a bridge in the scroll. 'It's amazing,' Sara whispered to Lily, and Lily nodded. 'What's happened to that ship?' Lily whispered, looking at the screen.

Sara shrugged, unsure. She was just about to put up her hand when Ms Ling pointed to the ship and said that because the river was fast-flowing and difficult to navigate, the ship had got into trouble – its mast becoming entangled in the wooden struts below the Rainbow Bridge. As a result, the people on the riverbank were heaving on ropes, trying to pull it free.

Sara could see the strain on the people's faces as they pulled, hear the rushing of the river and the creaking, complaining timbers on the ship and bridge, smell the muddy water and the dusty air, feel the crush of the crowds and the heat of the springtime sun…

'So real…' Sara whispered, eyes wide. 'So unbelievably real…'

At the end of the lesson, Ms Ling switched on the lights again. Sara looked around. The rest of the class looked sleepy – but Sara wanted more. She couldn't wait to see the real scroll when the class visited the Beijing Museum tomorrow.

'Alright, everyone – pay attention, please. The bell is about to ring. Before it does…'

Lily leaned over, and while Ms Ling was addressing the class, she whispered into Sara's ear from the corner of her mouth, taking care to keep her eyes on Ms Ling. 'Are you coming to the Lufthansa mall tonight?'

Sara bit her bottom lip. She had completely forgotten about Annette's birthday party. Annette's father, who worked in one of the big foreign banks in Beijing, had missed her actual birthday because he was in a meeting in New York. He was always doing that. After returning from the USA, he had promised to take Annette and her best friends from the Palm Springs development – Lily, Zafira and Sara – for pizza at their favourite mall. Sara was dying to go, but it wasn't quite that simple. There was a problem, and the problem was that she had promised to visit someone else this evening, even though she didn't really want to.

Granny Tang.

Sara couldn't wait to fly to the UK and see Granny Livingstone, her father's mother who lived in London. Granny Livingstone was always laughing and joking. Her other grandmother, Granny Tang – her mother's mother – was completely different. To begin with, she was 130 centimetres tall and lived in the same apartment building as Sara did. So not only did she see Granny Tang almost every day, Granny Tang was always asking her about her grades and her school reports, always pushing her to 'do better' and 'try harder'. In fact, that was all Granny Tang seemed to talk about. Well, that and how important it was to respect one's elders. To tell the truth, Sara found it pretty boring. Not that she didn't love her grandmother – she loved her dearly – but if she was honest, she spent most of the time in Granny Tang's apartment thinking about cunning ways to get out of there as quickly as possible.

Lily was still waiting for an answer about the party.

Sara sighed. 'Let me think about it.'

# CHAPTER 4

━

'Were those idiots bothering you again?' Joaquin asked.

School was over and Sara, Lily and Joaquin were in the corridor, bumping along with everyone else as they made their way to the buses. As she turned to answer Joaquin, one of the notes on the noticeboard over Joaquin's shoulder caught her attention. Untidily written with a black Sharpie, it was advertising the position of deputy editor on *Today!*, the school newspaper.

'Sara?' It was Joaquin. She didn't need to ask which idiots he was referring to.

'I don't pay them any attention, to be honest.' As soon as she said it, she knew it wasn't exactly true.

Joaquin raised his dark eyebrows. 'You, my friend, are *muy paciente*,' he said as the three of them burst out of the dull corridor with its chilled air and into the bright sunshine and humidity of a Beijing afternoon. They strode towards the waiting buses.

'Very patient? Her?' Lily cried, pointing. 'No way!'

'What?' Sara said. 'I'm very patient…' Even Sara could hear the feebleness in her own voice.

'Yeah, right. I see your face when the Ferdinand brothers are being annoying. You look like you want to punch them. And…' Lily insisted, cutting off Sara's objections, 'don't even mention hangry.'

'Hangry? What is this word?' asked Joaquin.

'I don't get hangry!' cried Sara, laughing because she knew it was true.

'You do! You know you do!' Lily turned to Joaquin. 'It's when someone doesn't eat – if they are hungry, and they get grumpy – annoyed, angry,' she added, seeing the look of puzzlement on Joaquin's face. 'But as soon as they eat, they are fine. That's being hangry.'

'I see. I see. But I am also hangry, you know? I must eat, otherwise…' Stepping onto the bus, he turned his head and bared his teeth. 'I also am a crazy person.'

'Get on the bus, crazy person,' Sara laughed, pushing him.

Still laughing, the three friends went towards the back of the bus, past The Gerbil, Jaz, the Ferdinand brothers and all the rest.

'Only one more day of term! Where do you go for summer?' Joaquin asked Sara as they sat down on the last remaining seats. 'Your grandmother?'

Sara nodded. 'I'm going to Scotland first with my parents, then we'll go and see my father's mother, Granny Livingstone, in London.'

'I wish I was travelling,' said Lily. 'I want to go to Italy. I want to eat pasta and stroll around the Colosseum sipping espresso. *La dolce vita! Bellissimo!*

Sara laughed. 'I don't think that's allowed!'

Lily gave a who-cares shrug. 'How about you, Joaquin? Where are you going?'

'I fly to San Salvador airport. My family home is not far from there. I have many cousins, many uncles, many aunts.' Joaquin waved his hand as though the list of relatives went on and on and on. 'We meet and it is good. But this year, I want to do something special.'

'Like what?' asked Lily, raising her voice above the chatter of everyone else and the engine roar as the bus juddered and spluttered out of the school campus and into the traffic streaming towards downtown Beijing.

Joaquin smiled sadly. 'Near my house, a company is making many problems for… how do you say… wildlife?'

'What kind of wildlife?' Lily immediately asked. Sara knew Lily was interested in animal welfare and planned to become a zoologist.

'El Salvador is famous for many animals, but on the beaches the turtles are dying because of…' Joaquin mimed the action of digging. 'What is the word?'

'Building?' Lily suggested.

'Mining?' Sara said.

'Yes! Yes! Mining. In my country a mining company has built a *muy grande* plant near one of the beaches. It's a big problem because the animals from the sea, the turtles – in English, you say "leatherback" – cannot lay their eggs. And if they cannot lay their eggs, they will not survive.'

'That's terrible,' Lily said. 'Really awful!'

'What are they mining?' Sara asked. 'And why did they build there?'

Joaquin shook his head. 'No one knows how this company got permission or why it is building on a beach. Some say they dig at night and bring material from Izalco volcano to their place. Some say the process… the processing needs lots of salt water. But no one is sure.'

'What's special about the Izalco volcano? Why can't they go to another location that doesn't endanger already endangered species?' Lily asked angrily.

'All I know is that Izalco volcano has one thing you can find nowhere else: fingerite.'

'Fingerwhat?' Sara asked, her laugh dying as soon as she saw Lily's glare.

'Fingerite,' said Joaquin, his face echoing Lily's. Sara felt her cheeks glow a little. Joaquin continued. 'It is a very rare mineral

– rarer than red diamonds. Izalco volcano is the only place in the world you can find it.'

'But what is it used for?' Sara asked. 'The company that built the plant must need it for something, right?'

'As I said, nobody knows.'

Lily clenched her fists as she leaned forward, practically shouting. 'But your father is the ambassador to China. Can't he do something about it?'

'No, he can't,' Joaquin said. 'Yes, of course he is a diplomat, but...' He rubbed his index finger and thumb together. Sara and Lily knew what he meant. 'The plant brings many, many jobs, much investment. It's not easy to fight for turtle eggs when people need jobs.'

The three friends sat in silence for a moment as the bus thundered along, passing shops and cyclists and cars and trucks.

Finally, Lily said, 'So what are you going to do?'

Joaquin grinned widely. 'You know that Confucius said: "A journey of a thousand miles begins with a single step". I will take a single step.'

'Okay, so what's your single step?' Lily asked, adding in a low voice, 'And it was Laozi, not Confucius.'

Joaquin's laugh was a bark. Eyes shining, he pushed a strand of his curly brown hair away from his face. 'I have already taken my first step: I have found out the name of the person who owns the mining company.'

'How does that help?' Sara asked.

'Knowledge is power! I know the owner's name, so I researched him – *un poco*. It's not easy: he has many shell companies – many fake places to cover his tracks.' Joaquin laughed. 'But I will be like a hunter. I will follow him, find out why he needs the fingerite. If I can know that, I can know where he is... soft?'

'Vulnerable?' Sara suggested.

'Yes! Yes! Vulnerable. Maybe I will make a lot of bad news about him. Make a campaign, you know?'

'Who is he?' Lily asked.

Lily was almost as excited as Joaquin, and a thought flashed through Sara's mind. *Why aren't I? Why aren't I as interested as they are about saving turtles?* And the answer that came back was one she didn't like but couldn't deny. She hadn't joined school clubs, signed petitions, or got involved in environmentalism because she believed – deep, deep down – that nothing would make a difference. One person's actions would not – could not – change the world. So why try? She admired Lily. Lily was always fighting for what she believed in. But if Sara were being really, really honest, she also felt that Lily and Joaquin were wasting their time...

Without answering Lily, Joaquin dug into the bag that was lying at his feet. When his face reappeared, he was holding several pieces of paper. 'Wait,' Joaquin said. 'I will show you his face.' Joaquin unfolded the papers and held them towards Lily and Sara. 'This is him.'

Sara stared at the same black and white photograph from her father's paper this morning. It looked like a young man with an old man's wrinkled and worn skin, but the face was changing: its eye sockets grew bigger and darkened like chunks of coal, its chin dropped like a loose hinge, its lips fell from its mouth, its skin sagged like melted plastic, and its hair dissolved. Where a face had been before, a gaping, swirling chasm now beckoned. Sara gripped her seat, but it made no difference – a dark gravity was pulling her, sucking her closer. Before she could scream for help, she was inside the void.

# CHAPTER 5

Sara gasped. Was she underwater? Her body had instinctively taken a deep breath, as though it had plunged into a freezing sea. But she was standing on a hard surface.

'Help me!' She barely recognised her own voice, it sounded so far away, so weak. 'Help!' she cried more loudly. Were her eyes open? It was so dark, she couldn't be sure. She blinked – once, twice, three times. Then she felt it again: a presence. Something behind her.

She spun around.

Nothing. But the presence had moved.

'Who are you? What do you want?' She turned again, only just stopping herself from screaming.

Nothing.

Heart thundering, she stared into the darkness. Like black water, it shimmered and danced in front of her. She took a step back, all the while moving her useless eyes – left, right, up, down – and kept going, back and back until the heel of her foot struck a wall behind her, followed by her shoulders and the back of her skull.

Still staring into the glistening blackness, she reached a shaking hand behind her back. Cold, cold stone – and carved dragons. Nowhere to go. Her fingers searched the wall for a door, for a handle, for a weapon, for anything that might help her. But as her fingers raced along the wall, a light – at first dim and refracted like a distant star but growing brighter – shone in the darkness in front of her. For a fraction of a second, she relaxed a little. But what came out of the light froze every muscle in her body.

A spectre – the face of a boy about the same age as her followed by his weightless, floating body – drifted towards her, and out of the boy's mouth a tongue unfurled, probing and parting the air like a serpent. Sara had no breath with which to scream. Twisting and turning gently, the boy grew closer. The boy's hand reached out. She caught a glimpse of something on his arm. Then the nails on his thin fingers, long and curled, clawed the air. Behind them, eyes – just holes as dark as pits – burrowed into hers.

Suddenly, she found her breath. She screamed and clamped her eyes shut, pressing her cheek hard against the stone wall.

A name was whispered – like the sound of a breath released. 'Shaaan Wuuuuu.'

*Enough! Enough!* Shaking, sobbing, mouth pressed tight, eyes still closed, Sara slapped and punched and kicked, yet hit nothing. Then a cold wetness rose up her chin, dragging roughly across her cheek, slipping onto her eyelids…

'Sara? Sara? Hey!' Lily clicked her fingers in front of Sara's face. 'Anyone home? Yoo-hoo!'

'I'm here,' Sara said and grabbed Lily's hand. 'I'm *here*!'

'Er… You okay? You look a bit freaked out,' Lily said.

'It's a genetic condition,' Joaquin said.

'What?' Sara said, still trembling, still getting puzzled looks from Lily.

'This guy,' Joaquin said, pointing to the newspaper cutting, where the picture was, thankfully, just a picture. 'He has a genetic condition. He's only seventeen but he looks fifty, or…' Joaquin gazed at it again and grinned. 'Okay, maybe sixty.'

'What? You're telling me someone who is only seventeen years old owns a mining company? That's crazy! Who is he?' Lily asked.

'His name is Chan and it's not just a mining company. His company, Bai Lu, has interests across the world – from farming in France to semi-conductors in Seoul.'

'Wow! How come I've never heard of it?'

Joaquin shrugged. 'I also didn't know him.'

The bus chugged through the traffic and as Sara listened to Joaquin and Lily talk more about Bai Lu's media profile, Chan's investments, tax havens, shell companies, pollution, and all sorts of other stuff, her heartbeat and breathing slowly returned to normal. What had just happened to her? One minute she had been looking at a photograph in a newspaper, and just like this morning at breakfast, the next she was in some cave with a *totally* freaky individual floating towards her. Not normal… In fact, that was a long, long, *long* way from normal. Okay, so she could sort of enter into things – like scenes in really good books or like today when she imagined the scroll as Ms Ling talked. So what? Everyone could do *that*! But to be swallowed by a face? To go into a scene against her will? That had never happened. And for that matter, she had *never* had floaty boys with serpent tongues appear in front of her, not even in her worst nightmares. Was she going crazy?

She released Lily's hand. Lily didn't notice – she was too busy emphasising a point to Joaquin about the disadvantages of fracking. Sara surreptitiously examined her own hand. It trembled. Then the image of the boy floating towards her appeared in her mind's eye again and it trembled more. She shook her head.

*No! Get a grip! Think of something else,* she ordered herself.

The advert for the school newspaper flashed across her mind. She could try. What harm was there in trying? She shook her head. True, she liked words. And true, the advert had unexpectedly caught her eye. But look at Joaquin and Lily! Now they were talking about marine pollution and the differences between zooplankton and phytoplankton! What did she know about such things? What did she know about *anything*? She slumped forward in her seat and, cupping her chin in her hand, watched as the world beyond the bus's dirty windows flicked past. She had nothing to say. Nothing to add to the conversation. But these were issues that everyone should be interested in, weren't they? Of course they were. If she made an application to the newspaper, it would be laughed at – *she* would be laughed at. Even thinking about doing it was a joke.

Depressing but true.

But right now, she had other things to worry about.

She was sweating, fighting her brain's desire to remember. She struggled to focus on something else… and lost. Immediately, images from that dark place filled her inner eye. Once again, she saw the floating boy – his vile, contorted grin, his disgusting nails, his empty eyes. Terror fired a shuddering jolt down her spine.

# PART 2

# CHINA
## NORTHERN SONG DYNASTY
## 996 CE

# CHAPTER 6

━

The valley – with its grassy lower slopes and its jagged, stony summits – funnelled the words so that when Shan Mu heard them and looked up, searching for his mother, he was surprised to see her standing far in the distance, waving to him. For a moment, he thought about waving back. Then he glimpsed the swirling, rising dust cloud in the distance and realised his mother was not greeting him, but warning him. He felt the growing rumble of the horses' thundering hooves; he heard the whoops and cries of riders.

'Shan Mu! Take Shan Tuo and run! DO YOU HEAR ME? RUN!'

Sheltering his eyes, Shan Mu watched the ten riders roaring past the furthest fields. Even from this distance, he knew who they were: Baojun's men.

'GO TO THE RIVER!' his mother cried. 'LEAVE!'

But Shan Mu did not move. And the reason was simple. They had seen him and would happily chase him down like a dog if he ran. Killing was these men's sport. As he watched, the riders reached the nearest fields. Sunlight glinted from their swords and off the gold they wore around their necks and arms. Some of the village men, his father included, were running towards the village, hats pulled off, sickles and scythes thrown to the ground.

By the time the riders entered the village, the villagers had scattered like startled fish, fleeing to the safety of their huts. Laughing, half-hidden in plumes of dust, Baojun's retainers dismounted.

Shan Mu had watched them. Then, not running but walking, he had grabbed his younger brother, Shan Tuo, and taken him to their hut. Crouched on its hard mud floor, bodies pressed together, they listened as the retainers began shouting orders.

'LET US SEE YOUR FACES!'

'EVERYONE OUT!'

'MOVE IT!'

Different, ugly voices shouting.

Shan Mu whispered calm words in his brother's ear. Shan Tuo was terrified; Shan Mu could feel his body shaking, could sense the river of terror flooding through him and drowning every other thought. Breathing slowly, Shan Mu wondered why the men had come. It must be for food. The weather had been bad and the harvest poor for everyone, including Baojun and his men. But even though the village's winter provisions were low, the retainers would not hesitate to leave the villagers short of rice. They had done it before.

A great tremor shook his brother's body. Although Shan Tuo was only 11 years old – four years younger than Shan Mu – he had the appearance of a much older man. His hair was thin and though his face was not ugly, it was lined and tired-looking. Shan Mu closed his eyes, his mind moving to the place beyond, the place that let him see the thoughts of others, that let him speak to them without utterance.

'Be calm, dear Shan Tuo. Be calm.'

In the corner of the hut, Shan Tuo's cricket rubbed its wings and chirped, oblivious to the danger. Eyes still closed, still in the place beyond, Shan Mu amplified the cricket's song, made it swim stronger in his brother's mind, raised it above the terror.

'Listen to the cricket, my little brother. Listen how sweetly it sings for us.'

Shan Mu smiled. It was easy to move into Shan Tuo's world beyond. Back in the hut, in the world of things, he simultaneously felt the tension in his brother's narrow shoulders lessen, heard his rapid breathing slow down and be replaced by deeper, more contented breaths…

The door burst open. Shan Mu opened his eyes. His mother – panting, wild-eyed – flew in, followed a moment later by his father, who quickly shut the bamboo door tight behind him. They rushed to the boys. The parents smothered them in their arms. Shan Mu closed his eyes, this time in pleasure. The love of his parents, the warmth of their bodies, the force that radiated from them, was fierce.

Suddenly, two men barged in. They grabbed Shan Mu's father and pulled him to his feet. 'Get up! Get up!' they cried. Shan Mu's father did not resist. He stood, head bowed, not looking the men in the eye.

'What are you doing here? What do you want?' Shan Mu's mother shouted.

The taller of the two men, a man with a scar that twisted across his eye and cheek like a crooked river, laughed and swung back his leg towards Shan Mu's mother. His father launched himself, knocking the man to the ground. For a moment, poor farmer and veteran retainer fought, rolling and struggling on the bare earth, but then more of Baojun's men came and after they had broken Shan Mu's father with their kicks and punches, they took him out of the hut, dragging him by the hair to where the rest of the villagers had been herded. Behind them, Shan Mu and his weeping brother and mother followed the red trail staining the dirt.

At the centre of the village, the man with the scar raised his arm and waited. There was silence and every villager's eyes were on him. 'As you know, Baojun, our lord, your protector, is engaged in battle in the north, ensuring that you,' the man pointed at the villagers, 'are safe from the bandits and robbers who roam these hills.' The man grinned. 'But, my friends, this is difficult and dangerous work that we do for you! It's also hungry work. We must be fed! We must stay strong! Is it not so?' The man waited.

Silence.

He nodded and drew his sword. The noise as it slid from its scabbard was like a snake slithering through dry grass. 'When we come here, we come as your saviours! Why do you not understand this? Why do you not treat us well? Why…' he said, raising his sword, 'do we have to put up with dogs like this?'

The sword flashed. When it fell, it sliced through the air and struck the neck of Shan Mu's father with a cleaving, destroying force.

# CHAPTER 7

—

Shan Mu was neither ice nor mist – not a part of the world of things or of the world beyond. He gazed empty-headed at the scene unfolding in front of him. Shan Tuo pulled at his sleeve, raised his tear-streaked face, wailed, 'Father.' As Shan Mu looked down on his younger brother, the world – his world – hardened, and an understanding of the force that moved it formed with crystalline clarity in his mind.

His father lay crumpled and motionless, the sword that had struck him glistening and dripping crimson. The murderer laughed and strutted with the other nine retainers, all brandishing their swords, raiding the stores and haranguing Gong Liu, the head of the village. His mother, lifting his father's head to her lap, wiped his face whilst Shan Tuo stood beside him and screamed and screamed.

Shan Mu straightened his back and scanned the scene: his terrified neighbours bowing so low that they scraped the dirt with their foreheads; the powerful retainers taking what they wanted from the winter stores, filling sack upon sack with precious rice, loading them onto their horses. Now he saw. Now the soft, translucent veil cast over his childhood by his parents' love was utterly gone. There was only one truth: strength, and only strength, mattered.

Shan Mu reached out a hand and gripped his brother's shoulder. His brother had taken a step forward, ready to run to where his mother was pounding the ground beside his father's body, throwing handfuls of dust into the air above her and cursing the retainers.

'No!' Shan Mu said in a voice that he barely recognised. 'Do not move!'

Shan Tuo looked up at Shan Mu and, though his cries went undiminished, he obeyed.

A searing anger was welling up in Shan Mu. He closed his eyes and stepped into the world beyond – but this time it was transformed. Gone were the fields of endless crops, the mountains that shimmered distantly in the heat, the cool breeze that rustled the trees. This time, a rollicking sky glowed red and in the air, veins were spreading wildly, running in all directions like the deep cracks of a dried-up riverbed – multiplying, dividing, deepening. Through the cracks, Shan Mu saw what he was looking for: the retainer with the scar. Extending a hand, he ordered his mind where his finger pointed. He would squeeze the man's brain. He would order him to raise the sword that had killed his father. He would have the man plunge the sword into his own belly. He would make him do it again, and again, and again…

Shan Mu stood, rooted in concentration. But then he staggered back, surprised. Then, angry and furious, he tried once more. But it was the same. He could not climb the wall that lay between him and the mind of the man he wanted to slaughter.

Frustrated, Shan Mu opened his eyes. The retainers were carrying away the last remaining sacks to their horses. The man with the scar was standing with his back to Shan Mu, watching the rest of the retainers work. Shan Mu's mother was silently stroking his father's hair, peering at his face. Shan Tuo was still crying, but the sobs, though deep and wrenching, were not loud. Gong Liu, kneeling on the ground, his hands clasped below his white beard, was pleading with the man with the scar, begging him to listen, to have mercy.

'Please, sir,' Gong Liu said, 'we are poor villagers. Soon it will be winter. We cannot survive it without rice to sustain us. Please leave us some.' Shan Mu's best friend, Gong Wei, pale and shaking, stood next to his father whose bowed head was touching the ground.

The man with the scar ignored him. Standing feet apart, hands on his hips, he watched as the final sacks were lashed to the horses.

Now was the time, thought Shan Mu. He had tried and failed in the world beyond. Now he would have his revenge in the world of things.

Releasing his grip on Shan Tuo's shoulder, Shan Mu took off, launching himself on the balls of his bare feet towards the man with the scar. Seven scurrying strides brought him to the man's back. Hand already extended, Shan Mu wrapped it around the now sheathed sword that hung by the man's side and heaved on its grip as hard as he could. The sword was heavy, so heavy, but somehow Shan Mu found the strength. The hilt slid up. The tip of the sword cleared the scabbard. There was noise – a cry of surprise. Shan Mu saw what was coming but could do nothing; the man smashed his fist into Shan Mu's face. Shan Mu felt his head snap back, a white-hot pain exploding in his head. He floated up and backwards. The words 'I will kill you' fell with the blood that was pouring from his nose and his body crashed onto the ground.

The last thing he saw before the darkness overcame him was his father's arm and the oath tattooed on it. Dirt had covered some of the characters, but Shan Mu knew the short phrase – contained by decorative, serpentine shapes at the top and bottom – by heart. Many years before, when his father had been recruited into Baojun's army, Baojun had forced his men to have their oath to him tattooed on their arms. This way the men never forgot that he was their supreme leader and their loyalty to him had to be absolute.

'*Establish the hegemon*,' Shan Mu whispered, reciting the oath as he slipped into unconsciousness. '*Establish the hegemon.*'

# CHAPTER 8

—

Gong Liu was the first to die in the days that followed. His face, once round and happy, withered and shrank. Like the rest, he roamed near and far, searching for food, eating moss and even bark, trying to stay alive, praying for the weather to change. It was days before his body was discovered in the far fields. His son, Gong Wei, gave no funeral rites. How could he? He himself was barely able to walk.

On the seventeenth day of the snows, Shan Mu's mother and brother huddled together in their hut, trying to share the heat their bodies could not afford to lose. The rat Shan Mu had caught that morning was cooking on a small fire at the centre of the hut. The rat's body had barely been big enough to prevent it from slipping between the bamboo slats in the trap. Shan Mu didn't care. He had dispatched it quickly, started the fire, and cooked it immediately. Now its charred flesh, dry and grisly, was ready to eat. Taking his knife, he divided it into portions, pushing equal amounts of flesh and bone into three tiny but separate piles on the wooden plate.

'Eat,' he said, bringing the plate to his family, his voice barely a whisper.

Shan Tuo rose up and snatched his portion, devouring the meat and crunching the bones, but his mother refused once again, turning her head away to face the wall of the hut.

'We have food, Mother,' Shan Mu said. And he sat, waiting, holding the plate with his mother's portion on it while Shan Tuo eyed it.

Shan Mu looked at his brother's face – his gaunt, tear-stained cheeks and his ravenous eyes – and his mother, whose face was still turned to the wall. He offered his mother's share of the rat to Shan Tuo, who snatched it from the plate and gobbled it, eyes flashing. Shan Mu gave his brother a smile and put the remainder of the rat's meat in his own mouth.

Chewing carefully to make the morsels last longer, Shan Mu thought about the scarred retainer. He *had* to find him. Since his father's murder, his world beyond had changed. Before that time, before Shan Mu had tried to kill the retainer, the air in his world beyond had been sparklingly bright and on the horizon were grass fields of a vibrant green with a snow-capped mountain range in the distance. But now his world beyond had changed utterly. The cracks and veins he had seen when trying to enter the retainer's mind had multiplied furiously and through them, a smoky-grey mist had begun to seep so that everything was now hazier, less defined than before.

Come the dawn, he would chase down the retainer in the world beyond and try again to kill him.

# CHAPTER 9

---

In the half-light, wrapped tightly in a blanket, Shan Mu opened his eyes. He shivered and pressed against his brother's back, who was himself pressed against their mother. He had woken just in time. A few more minutes and he would get up and check. But not yet. He wrapped his arms around his deeply hollowed belly. Somewhere outside the hut, a lone bird sang. The only other sound was his mother's wheezing and his brother's gentle snores.

They were all lying near the centre of the hut where the fire had been, away from the walls and the thousand crevices and cracks through which the wind had breathed its stabbing, unstoppable cold. Shan Mu lifted his head. The fire was out. He wasn't surprised. Yesterday, he had only managed to collect a few sticks to feed the fire's yellow, selfish flames. All that remained of it, and of the food they had devoured, was a smear of soft, grey ash on the hut's floor and a lingering, smoky smell.

The night had been a long, long one, and Shan Mu had woken often. Each time, he had asked the same question: how long before the dawn? It was the time he found it easiest to enter the world beyond and remain there. He had fallen asleep again, slipping back into dreams where he wandered, without shoes or gloves or jacket, through high, snow-peaked mountains, or swam naked across deep, icy rivers.

But the night, and his dreams, were at an end. Now that the dawn was minutes away, his heart was beating faster. His failure before now to find the retainer, to even get close to him, had bitterly frustrated him and more than once on his return to the world of things he had cursed himself. But this time, this dawn, he would get his revenge. He would drive a sword into the man's heart and watch him squirm on the end of it.

Opening the door of the hut, he gazed out. The eastern sky was bright, the sun's first rays soaring. Quickly, he lay down again and, willing himself to breathe calmly, he emptied his mind, withdrew from the hardness of the floor, the roughness of the blanket, the stiffness of his frozen limbs. Slowly, he closed his eyes…

When he opened them again, he was in the world beyond.

'What…?' Shan Mu cried, startled.

Shrouded by the grey air and the dark veins that twisted and turned in it, a tall man stood on a hillock a short distance away, eyes locked on Shan Mu. The man was dressed in a long grey cloth wrapped around his body – like a monk, Shan Mu thought. However, the man's head was not shaved. And there was something about the man's face – not violent or cruel, but not serene or kindly either – that made Shan Mu doubt it. Over one shoulder, the man carried a small sack, tied at the end of a stick. Shan Mu watched the man watching him. There was a look on the man's face… A deep fold was buried between his eyes, and his lips were tightly pressed together as though he were trying to prevent himself from speaking hastily.

Shan Mu walked slowly towards him and stopped. The man still watched him, still frowned. For a moment, neither said a word, but then, growing impatient, Shan Mu asked, 'Who are you?'

'I am Tian Lan,' the man replied curtly.

'What do you want? What are you doing here? This is *my* world beyond.'

'I have come to speak with you,' Tian Lan said, pulling the small sack from his shoulder and setting the bundle down at his feet.

Shan Mu frowned. No one had ever entered his world beyond that he didn't know already or wish to see there. He willed himself to sound confident. 'Why do you want to speak to me?'

Tian Lan sat down next to the cloth bundle. He looked sharply up at Shan Mu. 'You,' he said, crossing his legs and raising his voice, 'have done this…' He waved a hand. 'You have poisoned your world beyond with your motives.'

'My motives? Who are you to question my motives?' Shan Mu spat out. A rage welled up in him. What could this man know of his loss?

Tian Lan bowed his head and slowly shook it. When he raised it again, the anger Shan Mu felt had melted away, and instead there was emptiness – a hollow, dull ache in his heart.

'You have a choice. There are many paths to contentment, do you hear me?'

Before Shan Mu could reply, Tian Lan held up his hand. The hard look in his eyes had suddenly softened. 'Go back, Shan Mu,' he said. 'We will speak later. Your mother needs you.'

Shan Mu opened his eyes.

Crouched over their mother, his brother was weeping.

'Mother?' Shan Mu cried, scuttling to her side.

His mother's breathing caught and faltered. Her eyes flickered open. 'Take care of your brother, Shan Mu,' she said in a whisper. 'You promise?'

'Not yet!' Shan Mu cried.

His mother frowned. 'You promise?'

Shan Mu, unable to speak, nodded.

'You are young. Only boys. I am sorry. I am so sorry…' A tear trickled down her cheek, pooling and swelling for a moment on her chin before it fell.

'Mother!' Shan Tuo cried, burying his face in his mother's arm.

Shan Mu gently pulled Shan Tuo away and held his head.

With his other hand, he closed their mother's eyes.

# CHAPTER 10

—

An icy coldness seized him. It burrowed and burrowed into his bones, all the way to the marrow, and when it got there, it did not let go. His mind began to float. He wanted to wake up at dawn, go to the land beyond, continue searching for the retainer. But he could not. He did not have the strength. Night became day with nothing in between except Shan Tuo's face – thin, scared, crying – sometimes hovering above him, sometimes not…

The fever had started two days after his mother died. At first, Shan Mu was almost happy – he no longer felt hungry, no longer ached to fill his belly. But then his muscles and bones turned to water so that he could not stand or even raise an arm. And he sweated. It dripped from his brow like rain and drenched his body.

*I will not die! I will not leave my brother!* he told himself.

A flash of lighting clutched the night for an instant before it was snatched away by the dark. The thunder and lashing rainstorm roared outside the hut. The icy wet wind slipped through the slits in the walls and under the door as Tian Lan struggled to keep a small fire going. It was hopeless, even for him. The wood gave forth more smoke than light, and no warmth. He shivered and tried once again. Hopeless.

Shan Mu, lying in front of him, moaned softly. His body was often gripped by intense bouts of shivering, his whole body shaking uncontrollably. Tian Lan knew that this was a door the boy must pass through alone; still, his fear and love for the boy made him draw near. He bent over to wrap the boy's robe more tightly around his frail body.

Tian Lan had never before encountered someone as powerful as this boy, someone with the same gift he had been granted: the power to walk in the other world, to see the warnings and advice it offered to the observant. This boy could do so much, could be so great a sage…

Tian Lan reached into his robe and took out the amulet. All these years he had carried it, but never had he needed its power as he did now. He placed the dragon-shaped stone disk on the boy's chest and laid his hands over it. Tian Lan closed his eyes and felt the light grow within his own chest. The light was transformed into sound, a song that he began to sing. The song echoed in the hut, growing louder. The amulet began to glow, growing brighter as Tian Lan continued his song.

The boy would need guidance: anyone with so great a power would. It was his task to guide the boy to the better path, to set him on the road he too had taken.

Tian Lan leaned over and whispered to the boy.

'Only by knowing temptation can we know ourselves. Only by knowing weakness can we know strength. Only by knowing nothing can we know everything.'

Shan Mu's limbs had stopped thrashing and he had begun to breathe more soundly. Tian Lan placed the amulet back inside his robe and thanked the gods for their help. Then he took his place at the boy's side once more and closed his eyes.

Despite the darkness, Tian Lan's body told him morning had come. He rose again, shuffled to the door and inched it open. Even as the wind and water drenched his flapping cloak, the rain seemed to be abating. But still dark clouds stretched to the horizon like a dirty shroud, blocking any sun. It stayed murky and overcast all day until the pitch black of night.

Tian Lan fought the urge to sleep, but the last four days had been too much. He slumped against the wall of the hut and closed his eyes. Shan Mu's loud moan woke Tian Lan. He quickly stepped over to Shan Mu's side and tried to enter the boy's mind but found it closed. With a pang of concern, he drew back, leaving Shan Mu to confront his inner demons. His own heart heavy, Tian Lan turned his back on the boy and added wood to the fire.

The sun rose the following morning, the sky a playful blue that only comes after it has been torn apart in a storm. The cheerful and busy twittering of birds ended Shan Mu's fitful sleep. Eyes still closed, his first thought was: *I am alive.* How long he had lain fighting the illness, he did not know. He would have to ask Shan Tuo. He rolled onto his side and opened his eyes. Sunlight from the open door fell across the hut's earthen floor with a dazzling, dizzying brightness. He shielded his eyes, and saw feet – an arm's length away, bound in wet leather.

Shan Mu slowly raised himself onto his elbow and stared up at the figure standing in the doorway. 'You!' he exclaimed.

Tian Lan nodded.

Shan Mu looked around the hut. 'Where is my brother?' he asked, pulling off the blanket. 'What have you done with him?'

Tian Lan did not reply.

'I want to see my brother,' Shan Mu said. Pushing past Tian Lan, he stood in the doorway and gazed out at the silent village, at the slushy snow piled against the huts.

'Shan Tuo!' Shan Mu called.

'He is not here,' Tian Lan said. 'There is no one here.'

Ignoring him, Shan Mu slipped and slid across the melted snow and rain puddles and entered every hut in the village. And in each one, he found the same thing: nothing. Where was everyone? What had happened to the rest of the village? Had they all died? Had someone taken them? When he struggled back towards Tian Lan, he was breathing hard, anger and exhaustion squeezing his lungs. 'Where is everyone?' What happened?'

'I don't know. But they are in a safer place.'

'How can you know that?'

'I feel it,' Tian Lan said.

'You *feel* it?' Shan Mu scoffed. His brow creased. 'Why would my brother leave me? He wouldn't do that!'

'Perhaps he had no choice. Perhaps he was ill, too, and was taken.'

Shan Mu's legs trembled and threatened to buckle. 'Shan Tuo…' he said.

'You are still weak,' Tian Lan said. 'But we must go.'

'I can't leave. My brother will come back here. I will wait for him.'

Tian Lan shook his head. 'Your brother follows a different path. We must go,' he said again, but this time more firmly.

'Go where?' Shan Mu asked angrily.

'There are armies to the north and south. If the weather improves, they will fight.'

'You did not answer my question!'

'We must go wherever the way takes us. Out of the valley,' Tian Lan said, pointing west.

Shan Tuo's worried, skeleton-thin face flashed across Shan Mu's mind. He felt a fathomless sadness. 'If I go west with you, will I find my brother?'

'I'm not sure. It depends.'

'Depends on *what*?' Shan Mu cried, suddenly furious again. Was this man playing games with him?

'On fate. On decisions made. On you!'

'I don't know what you are talking about. You make no sense.'

'I don't expect you to understand. Not yet, at least.'

Shan Mu glared at Tian Lan.

'Will you come with me?' Tian Lan asked, swinging the stick that carried his sack onto his shoulder, and without waiting for an answer, he strode away, his leather shoes splashing through the slush and puddles.

Shan Mu watched Tian Lan stride past the last hut. Shoulders drooping, he looked around his village. There was no food here. His mother and father were dead. The villagers and his brother were gone. Even if he remained, waiting and hoping that his brother would return, how long would he survive on his own? Even if he did not starve, what if there really were armies on either side of the valley? Wouldn't soldiers come and force him to join their army?

Tian Lan was nearing the first of the village's fields. This man had appeared in the world beyond… it meant he had power. Perhaps he even had the power to find his brother.

'Hey!' Shan Mu cried.

Tian Lan continued walking.

'Hey!' Shan Mu cried again, but when it was clear Tian Lan would not stop, Shan Mu ran after him. As he passed the near fields, his eye fell on one corner of them. Fresh mounds of earth. Shan Mu stopped. He counted twelve of them, each the size of an adult. He thought of his mother and father lying in the cold earth… He clenched his jaws together, refusing to shed a tear. Others would cry before he did, he told himself.

Exhausted and panting, he caught up with Tian Lan. Tian Lan's hand reached out, and Shan Mu accepted the rice ball he offered. He ate it without thanks. The taste he did not care about. It filled his stomach, nothing else. He gulped down the water Tian Lan gave him from a leather flask. Tian Lan wrapped a warm cloak around Shan Mu.

They walked in silence. After some time, Shan Mu asked, 'How far are we going?'

Tian Lan interrupted his whistling and said, 'As far as we need.'

'As far as we need,' Shan Mu repeated, mimicking Tian Lan's voice. 'Your words are like mist.'

Still striding on, Tian Lan turned briefly and grinned. 'Mist?'

'They hide more than they reveal,' Shan Mu said.

Tian Lan grunted. 'You will know more soon. As will I,' he replied.

'Who *are* you?' Shan Mu cried. '*Why* did you come to my village? *Why* did you appear in my world beyond? *Why* are you helping me?'

Tian Lan stopped so suddenly, Shan Mu crashed into his back. Dropping his stick and grabbing Shan Mu's arms, Tian Lan stared into Shan Mu's face. 'You are special, Shan Mu. Don't you know that? There are others like us, others who can travel to the world beyond. But you have a power like no one else. You must not…' Tian Lan stopped, blinked. 'I want to help you, is that so bad? Is it?'

Shan Mu pulled his arms free. 'I must not what?'

'You must consider your motives.'

'That was not what you were going to say.'

Tian Lan picked up his stick and swung it onto his shoulder. 'I cannot make your choices for you.'

Shan Mu almost laughed in Tian Lan's face. Choices? What choices? He had no choices! He *had* to find his brother. He *had* to hunt down every member of the retainers' families.

'We have far to walk,' Tian Lan said, gazing along the valley. 'It is best we continue.'

Shan Mu nodded. He would follow this man out of the valley. He would go that far, at least.

# CHAPTER 11

Shan Mu sat slumped on a dark rock. His feet ached and were bleeding from the long walk that had started at dawn. Now, it was early afternoon and they had stopped next to a river that flowed down from the mountains. When Tian Lan suggested making a fire, Shan Mu had tried to help, but almost fell from exhaustion. Tian Lan had carried him to the rock, laying him gently on it.

Tian Lan wandered along the riverbank, carefully picking a route through the boulders and occasionally reaching down and gathering up sticks. Tian Lan had walked fast, and many times Shan Mu had wanted to tell him to slow down. But he hadn't. He was determined not to ask any favours of him or show any weakness. For what he must do, he would have to be strong. He would show no mercy, so he should not expect it from others. He breathed deeply. The river splashed gently past. He had listened to Tian Lan talk, and talk, and talk. How peaceful the river sounded… His eyes drooped and soon they fell shut.

The warmth of the fire woke him up. It was late afternoon, the shadows a little longer than before. Tian Lan gave him some water.

When Shan Mu was sitting up, with eyes wide open, Tian Lan asked, 'Can I show you something?'

Shan Mu shrugged. Tian Lan reached into his sack and brought out a brush. He wetted it and on a flat, dry rock, next to Shan Mu, wrote 心.

When he finished, he asked, 'Can you read?'

Shan Mu shrugged. He knew some characters but not many.

'It is the character for "heart",' Tian Lan said. 'There is a reason why it is called a character. Every line – its weight, gesture and balance – is a map of the hand that shapes it, a reflection of the character of the individual who brings it to life. The way of the brush is more than notation; the written word holds our thoughts and feelings, our inner voice.'

Shan Mu gazed at the character. It did reflect something in Tian Lan's face: his strong jaw, perhaps.

As many moons passed and they continued their travels together, Shan Mu's memories of his village grew fainter. In the evenings, by the light of the fire, the old man taught Shan Mu to read and write. Shan Mu, an able student, learned quickly and soon he knew hundreds of characters, scratching them with a stick onto the dry mud floors of the caves they rested in or onto the caves' walls with invisible, flowing strokes of his fingers. He learned to read from the only book the old man possessed: *The Analects of Confucius*. Over and over, Shan Mu would read about how ren, true benevolence towards all people, could be cultivated through devotion to one's parents and respect for ritual. Shan Mu would read the pages, and he would try to bring the words of Confucius into his heart...

They would stop in beautiful forests. On these days, the air felt alive. It seemed to vibrate, thrum. A dense music – the call of birds, the buzz and chirp of insects, the whispering of trees – seemed to float on the wind and in this tapestry of sound, something would call his name... over and over again.

As they walked, Shan Mu thought less and less of the distance they needed to cover and more of their destination. He decided to ask the question that had gone unasked for too long.

'What is our purpose, Tian Lan?'

'Ah, yes. This is a good question,' Tian Lan said.

Shan Mu waited for him to continue but Tian Lan was silent. Shan Mu waited until he could wait no longer.

'Why are we travelling to the Kunlun Mountains?'

'It is a question to put to the Immortals. My path has been given to me in my dreams.'

Shan Mu was only partly satisfied by this answer.

'But what will I ask them? What will I say?' Shan Mu asked.

'That is something you yourself must learn.'

'Yes, but how?'

'You will know yourself in time,' Tian Lan replied. 'Find yourself in your actions. The river is in every drop of water that flows between its banks. Yet it only becomes a river by following its course.'

'Yes, but… ' Shan Mu began.

'What river do I follow? Where does my course lead?' Shan Mu asked. Tian Lan raised his eyes toward the horizon.

'Travel in the river valley is easier. There the sparrows live, most comfortably. Yet, to become far-sighted, to see as the hawk sees, one must face the challenges of the mountain peak. Each must choose.'

A thought flitted through Shan Mu's mind, one that he guarded from Tian Lan. To be a hawk amongst sparrows…

Shan Mu sensed a momentary cold shadow pass across his face, and then it was gone.

It was clear to Shan Mu that Tian Lan favoured the company of birds and trees over the company of people. During their travels, he never took them into villages, preferring instead to sleep outside under the leaves of willow trees or shelter in caves. It was usual, in good weather, for the two of them to lie down with the stars overhead.

One night, after snuffing out their small fire, Tian Lan asked Shan Mu to look to the heavens.

'Tell me what you see,' he said.

The sky was clear, the air crisp. Shan Mu, lying on his back with his head cradled in his hands, looked straight up at the glittering lights above.

'More stars than I can name,' he said. 'Or even count.'

'Yes,' Tian Lan said. 'The Heavens make our struggles down here seem very small indeed.' He paused. 'Yet, despite their great distances, we can know them. In ways that we only dimly understand, the Heavens govern our behaviour. It is for this reason that the shaman must know the astrological signs that support and generate one another in the great balance between Yin and Yang, Earth and Heaven.'

'These,' he said, waving his hand across the sky, 'are the Three Enclosures. To the North is the Purple Forbidden Enclosure. To the East, the Supreme Palace Enclosure, and the Heavenly Market lies to its West and South.' He pointed to the Western Heaven. 'And there, next to the Lake of Jewels, is the Jade Palace, home of the Eight Immortals.'

'You have told me of them,' Shan Mu said. 'How is it that they are immortal?'

'Legend has it that there is a fountain from which flows a water with an elixir that sustains them. This is a gift given them for their service to the Tao. Each of the Eight Immortals has earned a place in the Jade Palace by bestowing life or destroying evil.'

'Have you ever sought them out? Have you ever travelled to the Jade Palace?' Shan Mu asked.

Tian Lan smiled. 'It is a place very few are privileged to see.'

Shan Mu persisted. 'But have you ever gone there?' he asked. 'Surely you are their equal.'

Tian Lan was silent. He gazed into the distance. At last he looked at Shan Mu and spoke, his voice low.

'It is important that the shaman knows his place in the world and acts accordingly.'

Shan Mu felt the weight of Tian Lan's gaze, felt as if the old man were trying to look inside him.

'We must not forget that the essence of the Tao is balance. The great must live in harmony with the small. Greatness takes many forms. You will see.'

'What if I am unable to do that which is required of me, Tian Lan?'

Shan Mu saw the concerned look on Tian Lan's face. This question had been weighing heavily on his own heart for some time.

'This is the question we all must face.' Tian Lan said quietly.

They continued on their way. As steadily as the passing of the seasons, Shan Mu's knowledge grew deeper. Shan Mu found Tian Lan an adept teacher and he was eager to learn all he could from him. Whenever paper and ink were available on their journey, they would practice calligraphy, grinding the ink stick in water and covering the paper with neat rows of characters using a horse-hair brush that had been given to Tian Lan. Over and over Shan Mu would practice. And when the last piece of paper had been covered, the last bit of ink had run out, Tian Lan would write with water upon stones and Shan Mu would be forced to copy the script before it faded and disappeared. Shan Mu slowly grew fond of Tian Lan. His heart lightened. His nights became peaceful.

# CHAPTER 12

—

One afternoon as Shan Mu was picking berries and watching Tian Lan gather firewood, he looked up at the enormous rocks near the bend ahead.

Someone was coming.

A moment later, three men trudged round the turn in the trail like weary ghosts. They were dressed in layers of cloth that covered their entire bodies, and had cloth wrapped around their heads too. Looking down, they spoke quietly to one another. And as they came closer, Shan Mu heard the rhythm of their speech. Their throats rumbled as they spoke. He had never heard such strange words. While he listened, Tian Lan quickly crossed the ground between them and the men. Now, standing in front of them, he held out his hand, spoke a few words and pointed to Shan Mu.

The men looked at Shan Mu. One reached into his bags and pulled out two balls of rice. He placed these in Tian Lan's open palm. Tian Lan bowed deeply. The men returned the bow. For some moments, they talked again, the men gesticulating and pointing. Then they departed. Shan Mu watched them go. Slowly, they receded, and with a final wave of a hand, they disappeared.

'The generosity of strangers is more nourishing than any food we eat,' Tian Lan said, returning and handing a rice ball to Shan Mu. 'I had no more rice and no clear path to follow. Those strangers gave me – us – sustenance and direction.'

Shan Mu said nothing.

Tian Lan continued. 'The merchants said there is a village a few hours' journey from here. We can make it there before nightfall.'

'What about the firewood you collected?' Shan Mu asked.

'I enjoyed doing it! And another traveller can benefit from my labour. Anyway, wouldn't you prefer to sleep in a hut?'

Shan Mu suddenly thought of *his* hut, *his* village, the empty winter stores, the cries of the starving villagers. 'You still haven't told me where the rest of the people from my village went.'

'No,' Tian Lan agreed. 'I haven't.'

'You also haven't told me where my brother is.'

'As I said, I only know they have followed a different path.'

Shan Mu clenched his mouth shut. In his imagination, he saw his brother and the remaining villagers trudging, single file, over the mountains, rope collars tied to their necks, sticks lashing their backs, commands yelled in their ears. Is that what had happened? Shan Mu could hardly say the words, fearing that just by saying them, he would make the possibility more real. But he had to know. 'Were they taken?' he asked.

Tian Lan gazed at his feet and after a moment said, 'The world is a sacred instrument. One cannot control it. The one who controls it will fail. The one who grasps it will lose.'

'I don't understand,' Shan Mu said impatiently.

'We must respond to the world the same way as grass answers the spring breeze.'

'I am not interested in grass,' Shan Mu cried, almost spitting the rice out his mouth. 'I am talking about people.'

'As am I,' Tian Lan answered. 'As am I. We cannot control the world. We must bend like grass to the will of fate.'

'You mean, we must accept whatever happens?' Shan Mu shook his head. 'I am not grass.'

Tian Lan's eyes narrowed. 'What you mean is revenge is more dear to you than life, that it consumes your heart.'

Shan Mu's mouth fell open. He had not mentioned his plan to kill those who had murdered his parents, yet Tian Lan, Shan Mu thought, had read him as easily as a book.

Tian Lan continued. 'Do not cut and burn when you can plant and grow.'

More words like mist! Yet as Shan Mu looked into Tian Lan's face, he faltered. Deep in Tian Lan's eyes, there was no mistaking the great kindness that buoyed his soul. Tian Lan's frown and tough face were merely the surface, merely the ripples on the lake. He might look irritable, he might grumble and grunt, but these, Shan Mu knew, were only minor noises. He was only a boy, but he was no idiot.

Shan Mu wavered. He slowly rose to his feet, the half-eaten rice ball still in his hand.

'It is better to love than hate. The first raises you,' Tian Lan said, gazing up at Shan Mu, 'and the other drags you down.'

For a moment, the words astonished Shan Mu. Was Tian Lan *deranged*? 'Do you expect me to love the men who killed my father?' he cried, eyes blazing, the words rushing out in a furious torrent. 'My mother died, my brother was taken and my village was destroyed! All because of them! And you talk about *love*?'

'I only ask that you consider your path. The hate you carry will lead you…' Tian Lan's words faded.

'Where? Where will it lead me?' Shan Mu asked, his two feet planted, his shoulders tense as though he were about to trade punches. 'Tell me!'

Tian Lan gently shook his head.

Shan Mu stood over him, breathing in short, angry bursts, waiting. Tian Lan did not look up. With a snarl, Shan Mu pulled back his arm and threw the remainder of his rice ball as hard as he could. It soared for a moment, dipped, splashed into the river, and was gone. Tian Lan's insistence that seeking revenge was not the path to follow angered him beyond belief.

'Let's go!' Shan Mu said, turning and marching away.

After a moment's hesitation, and with a deep sigh, Tian Lan stood up. Almost to himself, he said, 'Even mis-steps make a path, but it is not yet too late.'

For the next hour and a half, they walked, Shan Mu trudging behind Tian Lan. A small village came into view, a ring of twenty houses or so. As they entered the village, they were quickly surrounded by smiling villagers. Shan Mu looked into their thin faces, saw the way their robes hung loosely around them, noticed the ribs visible on the pigs that lay in the shade. The people greeted them warmly, speaking a tongue that Shan Mu could not make out. It did not appear that Tian Lan knew this language either.

'How can we beg from these people?' Shan Mu asked. 'They do not have enough for themselves.'

'They will be blessed for their generosity,' Tian Lan answered.

'But what good are future blessings when they are suffering now?' Shan Mu asked.

'We must accept what Heaven has chosen for us,' Tian Lan replied.

Before Shan Mu could reply, an old woman approached and bowed. Tian Lan bowed too. She pointed to one of the huts and laid two hands under her head. The word she said sounded to Shan Mu like 'sleep'.

Tian Lan gracefully accepted the offer.

It was time. On the other side of the hut, Tian Lan slept, his chest falling and rising, his snores filling the air. Somewhere in the village, a cockerel crowed. Laying his head back on the blanket again, Shan Mu closed his eyes and withdrew from the world of things…

The air was brighter than before. The dark veins were fainter and the grey fog was retreating.

Shan Mu was in an unfamiliar place. He was standing in a field ringed by tall, slender trees. A cool breeze gently bent the tops of the rustling grasses, making the entire field pulse with life. Across the field, he could see someone. He watched as the man strode towards him. Although the man was still half a field away, Shan Mu recognised him: Tian Lan.

'Shan Mu!' Tian Lan called, a broad smile crossing his face. Shan Mu felt his heart swell with happiness. A calm contentment washed over him. He waved and Tian Lan waved back, quickening his pace. But as Tian Lan moved towards Shan Mu, something in Shan Mu began to change. The ambivalence he had felt towards Tian Lan, the fear that Tian Lan would change him, was diminishing with every step Tian Lan took, vanishing from his body like water through sand. And in its place, something else was coming, something he knew was always there. He was not sure what. Not yet. He only knew he welcomed it.

'Shan Mu?' Tian Lan said, standing in front of him.

As Shan Mu remained silent, so the smile slid off Tian Lan's face. The air grew cooler. Shan Mu could sense something approaching – like a bear creeping through the woods towards him, or a storm swirling unseen behind him.

'Shan Mu?' repeated Tian Lan.

Then the storm was in him. All around him, the veins ran madly in every direction and the air darkened as though night was descending.

'I do not like that name.' Shan Mu heard the words fly from his own lips.

'I see,' replied Tian Lan, his head bowed like a beaten dog's, his shoulders curled like a pitiful old man's. 'And what should I call you?'

'Shan Wu,' replied Shan Mu, drinking the sound of the name. It was a name that fitted like the most glorious robe imaginable. 'Call me Shan Wu!'

'Shan Wu,' replied Tian Lan, whispering the words. There was a look of great sadness on his face. 'You have made your choice. Is there nothing I can say?'

Shan Wu smiled. 'Nothing. You have *nothing* to offer me.'

When Shan Wu returned to the world of things, he opened his eyes and stared at Tian Lan. The dawn sun bathed Tian Lan's face in its pale light, making him look infinitely older – the lines on his face deeply etched, his eyes heavily hooded, his skin sagging and lifeless.

But Shan Wu was on fire. His heart was bursting. The power he felt! The strength! His time was approaching and nothing and no one would stop him. 'I will not follow another's path. It is not enough to accept what is given. I must make my own way,' he told himself.

And so, while Tian Lan slept, Shan Wu crept out of the hut and took the first steps on what he thought of as his journey: to find his brother, the scarred retainer and his revenge.

He strode south out of the village, with Shan Tuo's face – wrinkled, frail, old before its time – in his mind. 'Don't worry,' he said, passing the last of the village's huts, 'I will find you soon, Brother.'

He didn't know he was walking straight into the Taklamakan Desert, nor that it was also known as the Sea of Death.

# PART 3

# BEIJING, CHINA
## THE PRESENT DAY

# CHAPTER 13

—

The bus slowed down outside Chao Yang Park and stopped. Sara bounced out of her seat, said a quick goodbye to Lily and Joaquin and, pretending that the Ferdinand brothers were invisible, hopped off.

Sara's home wasn't far, and she was glad of it; the afternoon air was heavy with humidity. At the same time, she was also glad to get off the bus and get away from that photograph in the newspaper. Normally she enjoyed Lily and Joaquin's company, but all they had talked about the whole journey was Bai Lu and fingerite and turtles and damage to the environment. And what had her contribution been? What had she added to the discussion? The answer was not a lot. She felt… irked. But not at Lily and Joaquin. They hadn't deliberately excluded her from the conversation. She felt annoyed at herself, at how little she had to say.

A picture of Granny Tang's apartment floated into her mind. Entering Granny Tang's place was like going back in time. Scroll paintings hung from the walls, landscapes of mist-covered mountains, birds perched on branches with fruit that looked ripe enough to eat, scrolls filled with columns of characters written in ancient Chinese. Red paper lanterns, red incense, red plates – everywhere red, the colour of good fortune and happiness. And every time, Granny would ask her if she had eaten. Not that the answer mattered. Granny would tell her she was too thin and bring in fruit, or steamed buns, or dumplings to the table. It was while Sara's mouth was full that Granny would begin telling her stories. Sara had been told the tales so many times she should have been able to paint a picture of the characters in them with her eyes closed. But in fact, she had rarely listened closely.

'When I was younger, I loved *The Monkey King*,' Granny Tang would say, starting one of her favourite stories. 'The Monkey King challenged the gods using a magic staff, one that he could make as large as a tree trunk or small enough to keep behind his ear.'

That was just one of the stories, but there were others, so many others…

Sara stepped through the doors of Apartment Block 4 and into the chilled air of its air-conditioned lobby. She crossed its marble floor, pressed the button for the lift and waited.

Another thing Granny Tang always asked about was Sara's calligraphy. Sara's mother first took her to calligraphy classes when she was five years old, but Sara later found out that Granny Tang had been behind it. Sara and her mother had argued about the classes on and off for years; their last argument had only been a week ago.

'I don't want to go to calligraphy class today,' Sara had said.

'Come on, Sara, you know how pleased you are with your work afterwards,' her mother had replied.

'You write beautifully,' her father had chipped in.

'It's Sunday. I've just had six days of school.'

'We've already talked about this, Sara. Granny—' her mother began.

'I know, I know. Granny's afraid I won't *develop a deep appreciation* for Chinese culture,' Sara shot back. 'I can write Chinese characters in the running, grass and seal styles. What more does she want? The next thing she'll have me doing is making paper or spinning silk,' she said, folding her arms.

'Sara!' her father said. 'Don't be disrespectful!'

'But I don't get any time to myself! When can I visit my friends, or go shopping, or practise the clarinet? I'm always doing stuff that other people want me to do. What about the things *I* want to do?'

Her mother had been furious but hadn't shouted – at least that had been a good thing. Eventually, after the silence her mother inflicted had become unbearable, Sara had gone to class, but she was sick of it. Sick of calligraphy classes, and sick of spending all her free time with Granny Tang.

By the time the lift arrived at her floor and its doors had opened, Sara had made up her mind: she wasn't going to go to Granny Tang's tonight. Instead, she was going to go to Pizzapie at the Lufthansa mall with the rest of the gang. Now there was only one question that needed answering: how was she going to do it? If she didn't go to Granny Tang's, her mum would find out and she would be in trouble – *big* trouble! There had to be a way…

'Is that you, Sara?' a voice called as Sara opened the apartment door and swung her schoolbag onto the floor.

'Yes, Mum,' Sara said. She waited. A moment later, her mum, book in her hand and reading glasses perched in her long, dark hair, walked out of the living room.

'Oh!' said her mum as soon as she saw Sara holding her stomach. 'What's the matter? Are you unwell?' Closing the book she was holding and stepping forward, Sara's mum placed a hand on Sara's brow.

Sara shrugged. 'My stomach hurts a bit. And I feel sick.'

'Oh, poor you,' her mum said, giving Sara a cuddle. 'Do you want something? A painkiller?'

Sara shook her head. 'Not really. I just… I just feel like sleeping for a while. I don't think I'll be able to go to Granny Tang's tonight.'

'Oh…'

'Is it okay if I lie down for a while? I don't really feel like eating anything right now.'

'I suppose so,' her mother said. 'Are you sure you're going to be okay?'

'I'll be fine, honestly.'

'I could stay a little later, postpone my 4pm class…'

'Mum, I'll be fine.'

'Well, it's just that Mrs Ching isn't coming tonight – her grand-daughter's ill.'

Sara nodded, making sure she kept her face neutral. What luck! Mrs Ching usually came and watched Sara when her mother was at work.

'I could ask Granny Tang to pop in and…'

'No need, Mum,' Sara said quickly. 'If I do feel better, I'll go down and see her.'

'Okay,' her mother said and looked at her watch. 'I suppose I'd better be going.'

Sara kissed her mother goodbye. As soon as the door closed, she danced along the hall: now she could go to the party and avoid another boring evening with Granny Tang.

In her room, she pulled back the door on her wardrobe. So many clothes. So many combinations. It wasn't a formal restaurant, but it was a birthday party. Would the others be casually dressed? What should she wear?

Choices, choices, choices…

# CHAPTER 14

—

Shortly after her mother left to teach her music classes at Xicheng Community College, Sara's father phoned. He was going to work late and wouldn't be home until after 9pm. Sara had almost jumped for joy. That part of her plan – how to get back home before her father returned from work at his normal time of 7pm – had been really bugging her. But now there was no need to worry because – hey presto! – the problem had been solved. Things often fell into place for her like that. She was lucky. Some people weren't. But she *definitely* was.

Sara chose a green t-shirt with the logo *10% human, 90% pizza* and her favourite pair of white trousers. Posing in front of the full-length mirror on her wardrobe, she looked at herself. She turned left and right but stopped.

What was that noise? Had a bee got trapped? She looked at her bedroom window. Nope, nothing there. Where was it coming from? She tilted her head and leaned towards the desk at the foot of her bed. The loud buzzing was coming from her computer. Why was it doing that? Her clarinet case was sitting on top of its keyboard. Was that why? She picked up the case. The buzzy sound stopped. She put the case back on the keyboard. The buzzy sound started again. She pulled the case off and pushed it under the bed. No more buzzing. Problem solved.

Looking in the mirror again, she smiled, sat down on her bed and called Lily – a last-minute check to make sure the arrangements hadn't changed. They hadn't.

A short walk in the canyons between the apartment blocks in the Palm Springs development brought Sara to Annette's home, and a short car journey with Annette, Annette's father, and the others brought them all to Pizzapie.

Tonight, she told herself, I'm going to forget all about what happened on the bus with that photo, and I'm going to forget all about having no idea about all the stuff that Lily and Joaquin talk about. Instead, I'm just going to eat pizza and have fun.

Annette's father, for the sixth time that evening, glanced at his heavy gold watch. When he looked up, he caught the waiter's eye and mouthed the word 'check'. Annette, who was sitting on Sara's left, was showing Zafira her new phone, which her father had given her as a birthday present.

So there Sara was, surrounded by three noisy girls and an uncomfortable-looking father in Pizzapie, having eaten great pizza, and chatted and gossiped for hours. Sara should have been feeling happy; she should have been having the time of her life. But she wasn't. She was miserable.

'What's up with you?' asked Lily, wiping mozzarella and tomato sauce from her chin and leaning back from the table.

'Nothing. Why?' Sara picked up her last slice of pizza, one with pineapple chunks, thought about eating it, but put it down on her plate again.

'You don't seem your usual self. Is it those Ferdinand brothers? If it is, I'll…' She clenched her fist.

Sara smiled. Trust Lily! Always ready to do battle! 'It's nothing. Forget it.' She gave a weak smile. 'Honestly.'

Sara unlocked her apartment door and closed it quietly behind her. 'Mum? Dad?'

No answer. She let go of the breath she was holding. Plodding into her room, she flopped onto her bed and lay there, staring at the ceiling with the lights off. After a few minutes, she got up, changed, and thought about reading. She gave up on that idea almost immediately, knowing she wouldn't be able to concentrate. She thought about playing her clarinet, but didn't stir.

Later, lying with her face in the pillow, she heard her mother come into her room. Pretending to be asleep, she was glad when the bedroom door closed gently and her mother's footsteps moved down the hall.

She closed her eyes. She opened her eyes. She twisted and she turned. One minute she was too hot, the next too cold, then too hot again. She kicked off the duvet, then, reaching down, she heaved it over her head, tucked her hands under her chin, and told herself to go to sleep. She groaned. It was no good. She slammed her head down on the pillow, then picked up her mobile.

It was 1.12am. She switched on her bedside lamp. It was going to be one of those nights. Sometimes she found it hard to sleep – like when she had exams the next day. It was her brain; sometimes it just would not switch off. But there was no exam in the morning, and there were no facts and figures running around her skull banging dustbin lids and shouting, 'Don't forget about me!' Instead, like a looped video in full colour, stereo sound, and ultra high definition, the scene in the hall and her mother's face when Sara had lied to her was playing again and again, just as it had all evening.

Her plan had succeeded brilliantly. She had gone to the mall, she had spent time with her friends, and she had avoided a long and boring evening with Granny Tang. The trouble was, she felt terrible.

She stared aimlessly at the lamp, at its unwavering light. But it wasn't just the lie that was bothering her. It was the bus ride home from school. Still. She wasn't jealous. That *definitely* wasn't it. It was the way she had felt. It was the way that Lily and Joaquin had talked about Bai Lu. They were so fired up about it, so ready to change things and she was so... There were lots of words to describe how she thought she must have looked.

*Apathetic* and *dumb* were just two of them.

# CHAPTER 15

━

Throwing off the duvet, Sara sat at her computer and began typing. Some aimless surfing would help, she told herself without really believing it. She typed in 'Martin Fröst'. When and where was his next concert? Martin Fröst, a Swedish clarinet player, was her hero. He was an *amazing* clarinet player. Frost's album, *Roots*, was one of her favourites. She also loved the idea that music could take the listener on a journey from ancient Greek hymns to modern music – a span of 2,000 years. Her mother had encouraged her to take up the clarinet when she was only five. Her father, not musical in the least, liked to hear Sara practising. 'Better a clarinet than a tuba,' was his little joke – one that Sara must have heard a million times.

There were no concerts planned for Beijing, but she clapped quietly when she saw he was going to play at Wigmore Hall in London over the summer. Could she get a ticket to see him while she was there? Her father hated classical music – Bad Money and other loud, rock bands like Tiger Reserve were more his thing. But her mother loved it – she would take her, for sure. As soon as she thought about her mother, the lie Sara had told her loomed up.

Sara closed the page and rapped her nails against the desk's hard plastic surface. What to look at now? Without thinking, she typed in the words *Bai Lu* and hit enter.

Immediately, she recoiled from the screen, pushing away from the desk as hard as she could with two hands, her desk chair skittering backwards across the floor on its three shaky wheels. She stared in horror at her computer screen where pictures from various webpages had appeared before she had quickly pushed herself away. She sat for a moment, trying to calm down. It had felt like something – the dark gravity she had felt while she was on the bus home, perhaps – had tried to pull her in, drag her into that place again with the floating boy. And she did *not* want to go there. For a moment, it was as though she had become a tiny piece of metal sitting next to a gigantic electromagnet. '*What* is going on?' she said shakily.

From three metres away, she stared at the search results. There were millions of hits, pages and pages about the company and about Chan. Nervously, she reached out a hand towards the computer.

Nothing happened.

She rolled herself a little further forward on her chair. A little further still. A little more. She stopped. That was far enough – with her fingertips, she pushed the mouse and scrolled. One result caught her eye. *Chan: The Boy Who Would be King* linked to an article written by a journalist working for *The Custodian* newspaper in Britain. She paused and raised her finger from the mouse. When Joaquin had shown her the picture of Chan, she had gone into that... place. What if seeing Chan, even just his picture, was doing something to her, freaking her out? What if he had some sort of supernatural power, some ability to possess souls – something like Sauron's ring in *The Lord of the Rings*? A shiver ran up her back. She shouldn't look at a picture of Chan. She should log off and get back into bed. The cursor hovered over the sleep option... But imagine telling Lily, who was scared of nothing, that she was afraid of someone's picture! No, this was ridiculous. She wasn't in the Shire, her neighbours weren't orcs, and Chan didn't live by Mount Doom! 'Calm down and stop being stupid,' she told herself.

The page with the article loaded. There was no picture of Chan. Relieved, she quickly scrolled down and read the first few sentences, all the time a feeling of unease growing in her. But it was impossible to stop reading, and she galloped onto the next sentence and the next. When she finished, she pushed her chair away and leaned back. She ran her fingers through her hair and looked at the time. It was nearly 2am. Switching off her computer and her bedside light, she hopped into bed and closed her eyes. Her mind was racing, her brain doing the Shanghai Grand Prix thinking about what she had read.

Chan was the youngest CEO in the world. Although he was only seventeen, he appeared older because of a genetic condition that caused premature ageing. He had recently bought an entire skyscraper in Kowloon, a place with some of the most expensive real estate in the world. The article didn't give details, but it seemed parts of Chan's business empire were under police investigation, which made sense given the way Chan had ignored environmental concerns to build his factory in El Salvador.

So, Chan was rich, a bit dodgy, and suffered from a rare medical condition. Nothing there to explain why her brain had gone nuts and thrown her into a dark place with a floating boy and carved dragons when Joaquin had shown her Chan's picture on the bus. It was puzzling and frightening and it was also so... random, so disconnected. She thought about the name she'd heard – Shan Wu. It was sort of interesting. The family name, Shan, was quite rare in China these days. As for 'Wu', that could mean a couple of things. As a family name, it meant 'martial and war-like'. But it also meant something else quite different. 'Wu' was the Chinese word for 'shaman', someone who could enter a trance and journey to the unseen world, someone who had influence over good and evil...

When she finally fell asleep, sometime after 3am, she dreamed of dark, neglected houses, of whispered half-heard words, and sly, creeping voices.

# PART 4

# THE QINGMING
# SCROLL
## c1162 CE

# CHAPTER 16

—

The students got dropped off at the Eastern Prosperity Gate – the nearest they could get to the Forbidden City. After walking for ten minutes beside the city's eight-metre high walls, they arrived at the *Wu men* entrance – the Meridian Gate.

Once inside the Forbidden City, home to Chinese emperors and their governments for hundreds of years, the small group of fifteen was led by Ms Ling through the crowds to where their guide was waiting, a shiny badge in his lapel and a bright smile on his face.

'Everybody here?' he cried. 'Good! Come on, follow me!' He shot away, urging them to follow. Sara was directly behind him, with Lily and Joaquin on either side of her. Jaz and The Gerbil, the Ferdinand brothers, and the remainder of the class were behind Sara, and Ms Ling at the very back of the group.

'Do you like Chinese art?' Joaquin asked her as they walked, or rather galloped, towards the entrance to the Palace Museum, which was nestled below tiered roofs.

'I love it!' she replied. 'You?'

'Sure!' Joaquin replied. 'The paintings are misty.'

'Misty?' Sara asked. She and Lily looked at one another, both equally puzzled.

'You mean there's a lot of fog in the pictures?' Lily asked.

'No, I mean they make a good emotion but there is something you don't know.'

Sara tried not to laugh. 'You mean mystical!'

'Mystical,' Joaquin repeated, nodding his head. 'Yeah.'

'Yeah,' Sara said, glancing at the smirk on Lily's face as they joined the back of the long queue to enter the museum.

Inside the museum, Sara caught a glimpse of a glass case but that was all. There were too many people to see much else and the guide, with arms wide open, was herding them together as though they were goats. When they were all in a tight circle, he pointed over their heads and cried: 'Look! Amazing, eh?'

Through a gap in the crowds, the spectacular scroll appeared, just a segment of the five metres that lay under the glass case stretching from one end of the room to the other.

'Well,' said the guide, 'take a few minutes to look at it in more detail. Then come back here and we can talk about what you think.'

Sara joined arms with Lily and together they stepped up to the glass case. Without warning, Sara's whole body started shaking uncontrollably. She tried shouting to Lily, but nothing came out. She stared at Lily in panic, but Lily was acting as if nothing was happening, gazing calmly at the scroll and chewing her gum. Every molecule in every cell of Sara's body was vibrating, thrumming. It felt like she was about to fall over. She tightened her grip on Lily's arm.

'What's the matter?' asked Lily, a little surprised.

Sara took three or four deep breaths. Her head was spinning. 'Nothing,' she managed.

Lily was about to say something when the guide spoke again.

'Gather round me,' the guide called. His voice seemed to come from a long way off. 'Gather round me,' he repeated. Sara shook her head. How weird she felt! Still clinging to Lily, she stepped away from the scroll and joined the rest of the class, who were standing a few metres away. As soon as she did so, the strange feeling began to fade.

'So,' said the guide, casting his eyes around them all and pointing a thumb over his shoulder towards the scroll, 'what did people in the past do when they wanted to look at the Qingming scroll? Did they put it in a six-metre glass case like this one? Hmm? What do you think?'

Although Sara knew the answer, and although the strange sensation had now gone entirely, she was feeling a little shy. The guide's words hung in the air. He paused, waiting for someone to speak. Ms Ling waited too. It was The Gerbil who eventually spoke up. 'Did they hang it up on the wall?' she asked.

The guide pursed his lips and gave a little shake of his head.

Sara scoffed. 'A six-metre scroll on a wall?'

The Gerbil shot her a drop-dead look, but even Jaz was smiling.

'Did they unroll it, a little at a time?' Sara asked.

The guide smiled. 'Very good! They unrolled it from right to left, looked at one section at a time, and moved onto the next. In other words, they rolled and unrolled as they went along. Good. So, let me ask you this: do you know the scroll's full name?'

The class nodded.

'*Qingming Shanghe Tu*,' said Francis Ferdinand, jiggling his eyebrows at Sara as if to say, 'See how clever *I* am!'

'That's right. But what does the name mean? Hmm?' asked the guide.

'Er…' replied Francis, making a face like he had just sucked on a lemon.

Lily didn't hesitate. '*Shanghe Tu* means "along the river" and *Qingming* is the name of the spring festival – the time when people sweep graves and burn incense so they can pay their respects to the dead.'

Tony and Francis looked disgusted. The Gerbil looked confused.

'Well,' said the guide, 'that's true. But some people think "Qingming" also means "peace reigns". Do you think it is a peaceful picture?'

Joaquin, who was standing between Lily and Tony and Francis, frowned. 'Not really,' he said. 'Everybody looks so busy.' Someone else disagreed and said the picture made them feel calm because there was lots of countryside. Then Xing spoke up, suggesting that everyone was minding their own business and going about their life quietly, so it was peaceful in that sense.

The guide's eyes shone. 'Well, that's very interesting, young lady!' he said. 'I'm sure your teacher has told you about Confucianism.' He paused. Ms Ling nodded. The guide continued, 'Do you think there is a connection between the painting and Confucianism? Hmm?'

Xing thought about this. The class thought about this too. Time ticked by. Jaz made a sound like someone snoring, which The Gerbil thought was hilarious – her stifled giggles turning her face bright red. And Tony Ferdinand had crossed his eyes and was swaying. But still there was no answer. The guide looked like he was about to give up when an idea popped into Sara's head. 'Is it that someone is sweeping a grave in the scroll and Confucius thought that rituals were important?' she asked.

'Oh, well done!' the guide cried.

Sara smiled. Then she turned and jiggled *her* eyebrows at Francis. But when the guide directed his next question to her, it was Sara's turn to look like she was sucking a lemon.

'And what did Confucius say about society? Or rather, what did the Neo-Confucians – such as Master Zhu Xi – say?' the guide asked.

'Er…' said Sara. She didn't really have an idea. She looked around her class; by the look of it, the others didn't really have much of a clue either – not even Xing.

The guide waited, but when it was clear that no one was going to take a stab at an answer, he spoke again. 'Alright, well, why don't you all go and take another look at the scroll. You can gather some evidence about why you think it is a calm or busy painting, and you can also think more about my question.'

To Sara's left, Lily and Joaquin were whispering intensely, locked in debate. To her right, Ms Ling and the guide were watching her and the rest of the class. Sara took a hesitant step towards the scroll. Then another.

She didn't manage a third.

# CHAPTER 17

**⸺**

She was on Extreme Rusher, the fastest rollercoaster ride in Happy Valley amusement park. Everything around her was turning upside down and round and round. She wasn't feeling faint, she didn't feel like she was moving at all, but everything else – the glass case, the scroll, the museum, Lily – was spinning, moving faster and faster and growing further and further away. She closed her eyes. But instead of seeing just darkness, she saw a strange glow. Colours began to appear, shapes of things… Trees, she could see trees. They seemed to be painted on the inside of her eyelids. More details appeared: clouds, people, a river. Where was this place? Where…?

Just as suddenly as the rollercoaster ride began, it stopped, and like a stone from a catapult, she felt her body being propelled through the air until – touch down! She landed face-first on something soft and lumpy.

Sara opened her eyes. Leaves? Yes, leaves… She was lying on a bed of thick, green leaves!

A crunching noise. Sara looked up. A man with dark eyebrows and a dark moustache was approaching, stick in hand, his brows knitted together.

'Wait!' cried Sara. Too late.

The stick hit her on the back of her shoulder, a stingingly vicious blow.

'That really hurt!' Sara cried angrily, jumping to her feet and rubbing where the stick had lashed her.

'Look at my cabbages! Look what you've done!' He raised his stick to hit her again.

'Are you crazy?' yelled Sara and, reaching up, she snatched the stick out of the man's hand, broke it over her knee, and threw the pieces to the ground.

The man stared at her for a second, his mouth gaping. Then he started yelling, ranting and raving about the damage and how someone would have to pay.

Sara walked quickly away – on tiptoes down the line of plants, trying to put her feet on soil and not on the green heads that covered most of the field; she really didn't want to harm the man's cabbages.

Behind her, the man was still yelling about reporting her. Reporting *her*! What a joke! When she was on ground that wasn't full of cabbages, she looked back. He had picked up a piece of the stick and was waving it above his head... but at least he wasn't chasing her.

She took a deep breath and... Wait a minute! How had she not noticed before? She was wearing sandals! Where did they come from? And rags! She was wearing rags that... She sniffed. 'Eeeew!' They stank! What was going on?

She looked around her but all she could see were fields, a river and trees. Her brow furrowed. She had no idea where she was, and yet there was something strangely familiar about everything. She began searching furiously through her breeches. Where was her mobile phone? Had she dropped it? She twirled, once, twice, three times. But there was no mobile. And there was no Ms Ling, no Lily, no Joaquin, and no Palace Museum – not even Tony and Francis Ferdinand!

She was in a beautiful, unknown place near a river. It wasn't very warm, though the sky was blue. Probably springtime... Her eyes opened wide. A river! Lovely trees! Fields! Springtime! A river! No way!

She slapped a hand over her mouth. The scream had already escaped.

The farmer looked up, shook a fist at her and went back to his cabbages.

'Oh no!' she said. 'O… M… G!' She felt sick. Had she really been transported into the past – somehow landed in medieval China and was now *in* the Qingming scroll? A wave of anxiety swept over her, swirling her stomach and choking her breath. 'Okay, okay. Take it easy,' she told herself. Bending over at the waist, she slowly filled her lungs, pursed her lips, and released the air, deliberately making as loud a hissing sound as she could. She straightened up, still feeling faint. She staggered but remained standing. She breathed in deeply again and released the breath slowly. Of course it was just a dream. It was the only sensible explanation. She was dreaming. And yet, everything was so… real: the wind on her face, the grit between her toes, the smell of the earth, the sound of galloping hooves.

'Look out! Get out of the way!' cried a voice behind her.

Sara swivelled just in time to see a horse and rider rushing towards her. She dived to the side, but the rider had already pulled hard on the reins – too hard: the horse heaved to the right, bucked, and tossed its rider violently onto the ground. The rider landed heavily, throwing up a cloud of dust, and after rolling several times, came to a halt at Sara's feet.

Sara stared at the old man lying an inch from her big toe. She was jolted from her panicking about her own situation. Was he hurt? Should she try to speak to him? His eyes were tightly closed and his mouth was pinched shut, which brought his wispy, white moustache to the tip of his nose. Before Sara could say a word, the old man opened his eyes. 'You stupid girl,' he croaked and spat.

'What did you just call me?' Sara froze. 'My name is Sara,' she said and clamped a hand over her mouth. Slowly, she released it. 'My name is Sara...' she said again. What was going on? She was speaking Mandarin! 'This is mad!' It was in Mandarin. 'I'm speaking Mandarin!' It was English in her head but it was Mandarin that was coming out of her mouth. 'I can't stop speaking Mandarin!' Granny Tang was always telling her to practise it more, and now she couldn't stop!

'Yes! Of course you speak Mandarin!' the old man shouted, then added, 'I think my leg is broken. Bring my horse to me.' He pointed over Sara's shoulder.

Sara hesitated. 'Don't you want me to...?' She moved towards the old man, ready to help him though she had no idea what to do with a suspected broken leg.

'Don't touch me! Just do as I say,' the old man yelled hoarsely, his face crumpling in pain.

'I understand,' Sara said, backing away quickly and looking for the horse. It was trotting towards the edge of the field, eyes on the cabbages. Before it could reach them, she ran over, grabbed the horse's bridle, and dragged it towards the old man, who was still lying on the dusty road, clutching his leg.

'Good!' said the old man. 'Now get the saddlebag off my horse. Come on! Come on! Hurry up!'

Something about not trusting strangers echoed in Sara's head but she found herself picking up the saddlebag off the horse and taking it to the old man, who was still flat on the ground.

The panic was welling up again. 'I don't know what's going on – I mean, one minute I'm in the Beijing Palace Museum looking at a scroll, and the next minute, I'm... I'm here!'

'You have to—'

'And where is here? It's definitely not where I was, is it? This does not feel right. Please help me get out of here!' She was almost screaming now. 'I have to get back to the museum. How can I get back? Will you help me to—'

'BE QUIET!' the old man roared.

Sara stared, open-mouthed.

'Do as I say, because if you don't, first they will kill me and then they will kill you.'

# CHAPTER 18

—

'Sorry, what did you say?' Sara asked.

'I said, first they will kill *me* and then they will kill *you!*'

'Who will kill us? What are you talking about?'

'The Gang of the White Fawn.'

'The *what?*'

'The Gang of the White Fawn!'

Sara was breathing faster and faster, her heart pounding in her chest. She was now really desperate to wake up from this nightmare.

'They want what's in the saddlebag,' continued the old man. 'You must take it and go! I will try to delay them. Promise me you'll take the saddlebag to Wan Yi. Promise it! Promise me you will take my saddlebag to Wan Yi, the silk merchant. Please! You will find her in Bianjing, which is only a short distance from here. Promise me!'

'Sir, I'm not sure I can help you. I don't even know if you are real, or if I am real. I have to get back to… my time.' She had no idea what year it was, but she knew it wasn't the 21st century.

'Sara, listen to me. This is real and we have no time to talk. You need to take the bag and run. We can't both die here.' Rivulets of sweat were making their way down his face. 'The woman you need to take the bag to is the most intelligent person in Bianjing. I can see you are very troubled. I can't help you, but Wan Yi will. You have to believe me. Please!'

Sara was deeply sceptical, but she realised she had no choice.

She had to follow this dream, wherever it was leading. She took a deep breath to calm herself as the man went on.

'Wan Yi knows all about weaving. Is not time woven? Can it not be stitched together and unpicked?'

Sara shook her head slowly, disbelievingly. She vaguely recalled a programme talking about Einstein's theory of a space-time fabric, which is distorted by the gravitational pull of large objects. So, was time a weave? Would a silk merchant called Wan Yi really be able to help her? She wanted to walk away, but what else could she do? There was no Siri, no Google, and no Wikipedia. All she had was this old man who was hurt and claiming his life was in danger. 'Where's her house? What's the address?' she asked.

'I don't know.'

'How can you not know?'

'I am a stranger to the city, and I have never met her before.'

'So, I am going to a city of… how many people?'

'Five hundred thousand.'

'You want me to go into a city of half a million people and find one person called Wan Yi. Just like that?'

The old man nodded. 'But Wan Yi is a merchant. She will not want to speak to a filthy urchin like you—'

Sara bit her tongue.

'—unless,' he continued – slyly, thought Sara – 'you have the saddlebag. Tell her Zhang Guolao sent you.'

*Where's the Wizard of Oz when you need him?* thought Sara. 'I see. Please give me the saddlebag, then,' she said. 'Don't I need to know what I'm carrying? Why would you not know where she lives when you are supposed to be delivering the bag to her?' That niggling thought in her head again about not trusting strangers.

Just then, a scream tore through the air. Sara had a lot more things she wanted to ask, but as she jerked her head up and glanced down the road, she saw there was no time.

Cloaks billowing in the wind, their horses' hooves pounding in the dust, seven riders were approaching. A man in a black cloak, fiercely urging his horse forward with his heels, was leading them. Behind the leader, six blue cloaks followed – altogether the most terrifying sight Sara had ever seen in her life. The rhythmic thudding coming from the galloping horses was travelling up her toes and ankles, making her knees tremble even more than they were already.

'The one in the black cloak is Mo Zei,' the old man said, his voice a terrified whisper.

Mo Zei had drawn his sword and was slashing at the air above his head, his thin face twisted in anger.

'Run!' Zhang Guolao said. 'Go!'

Sara took a step forward.

'Wait!' he cried, pointing to the saddlebag.

Sara grabbed the bag and ran – faster than she had ever done before. Off the road, behind the willow trees, up, up the hill – away from the men and their horses. One of her sandals flew off. She skidded to a halt, retrieved it, pulled it on, but didn't dare look back. She began running again, feet pounding, arms and fists pummelling the air. Her breathing became more and more rapid. She dodged between tree trunks, but she was slowing down, each step uphill harder to take. Her lungs were bursting. She couldn't keep going. She had to stop, get her breath back.

Behind her, the thunder of horses' hooves had stopped. The gang must have reached the old man. They would soon discover that he no longer had the thing they wanted. Then they would come after her. She had to do something – but what? Doubled over, she leaned against one of the willow trees and gulped down air, trying to douse the fire in her chest. Still gasping for air, she peered down through the trees to see if anyone was behind her.

The gang members dismounted their horses, slowly forming a circle around the old man. She couldn't see clearly but it seemed as though Mo Zei, the tallest of the seven, was twirling the tip of his sword in the air. Without warning, he stepped forward and kicked the old man three times. Zhang Guolao writhed. Another of the gang drew his sword, then another and another. They closed in, obscuring Sara's view. She couldn't watch, anyway. She wanted to throw up. Eyes closed, she heard the old man shouting something, then a single shriek, then laughter. She made herself look again, her heart hammering. The gang had moved away from the body as Zhang Guolao lay motionless, his head turned awkwardly to the side, a red ribbon of blood across his neck, a widening ring of crimson staining the dirt around him. She had never seen anyone die, let alone be witness to a murder. She was in deep shock, but despite it, and despite all her fears, she felt a rising rage. Why did they have to do that? Why did they have to kill him? She wanted to scream the question at the men. But her mouth stayed closed. If this wasn't a dream, if she had somehow travelled in time, she had to take care of herself. She had to. The question was: should she leave the bag behind and run? No! She should try to find the silk merchant. That was the sensible thing to do. Sensible! The word almost made her laugh.

Mo Zei returned his sword to its scabbard, raised his head, and scanned the fields where the farmer, oblivious to the horror, was still planting cabbages. Slowly, he turned his head... and stopped. He was looking right at the willow forest! He was looking straight at Sara!

She ducked behind the tree. Her heart was pounding. Had he seen her? She had to get out of there. But where? They had horses. They could easily hunt her down. A voice behind her made her jump.

'Come on! Put your back into it! We can't wait here all day.'

Sara turned in the direction of the shout. Not much further on, the woods gave way to a clearing. Beyond that, a small rowing boat was pushing away from the side of the river. The man in the boat was adjusting his oars while men in a ship, which was moored in the river about one hundred metres away, shouted at him.

She was a strong swimmer and this was the only hope of throwing the gang off her scent.

Sprinting across the clearing, she jumped into the water without checking its depth. Too late now if the contents of the saddlebag got spoiled in the water… The river had looked fast and muddy as she ran towards it, but she had no idea how fast or how muddy. She began swimming against the strong current to the little boat. She was already physically drained but adrenaline kept up her steady front crawl. She needed to keep her mouth shut or she would take a mouthful of the thick, brown water. The swirling current, like an invisible hand, pulled her below the surface. Kicking and thrashing her arms, she rose to the surface again. The blue sky shone briefly, then disappeared under the river's brownness. She threw her hands above her head, reaching for the sky. Her hands broke the water's surface and touched something – something solid. She grabbed onto it with all her might. Her head came out of the water. She was holding on to an oar.

'You crazy little fool!' she heard above the smack, tumble and slap of the river.

Sara had never been more relieved.

A strong hand grabbed hold of her by the neck and pulled. She landed at the prow of the little rowing boat like a newly caught fish and coughed up an awful lot of potato-tasting water. After a few moments, when she could breathe without having to concentrate all her mind on it, she checked she still had the saddlebag. Its leather strap, wet and heavy, was still around her shoulders.

Still coughing, she saw one of the men from the ship throw down a knotted rope, which the man in the rowing boat caught.

'Tell Little Pebble,' the man who threw the rope shouted, 'that if she can't climb up the side of our boat, we'll have to throw her back in!'

All the sailors laughed.

Sara looked up at the sailors and the side of the ship, whose dark wooden planks stretched up and up.

Hands and legs still weak and wobbling, she grasped the rope.

# CHAPTER 19

Sara had never climbed up the side of a ship before, and definitely would not have otherwise considered it when her arms and legs felt like water before she even started. Four metres above her, half a dozen heads were leaning over the side of the ship, bobbing about and chattering to one another.

'Come on, Little Pebble! We don't have all day,' cried someone with a voice of authority – presumably the captain.

Sara wiped a strand of wet hair from her face. Her rescuer had tied the little rowing boat tightly against the larger vessel and was staring at her. Sara ran her eyes along the rope, starting at the swaying end nearest her and finishing at the end that disappeared over the ship's railing.

The man in the rowing boat grunted and jerked his thumb up. Sara pocketed her sandals, amazed she still had them. The saddlebag was getting heavier across her shoulder, reminding her of the old man's death. Taking a deep breath and wrapping her hands around the thick rope, she eyed up the knots evenly spaced along it to the top. She started her climb.

Almost immediately, the rope swung forward and she smacked the ship's wooden planks with the soles of her bare feet. She fought away the desire to stop and rub them and instead focused all her thoughts on getting up the rope. But it felt as though her arms were being ripped out of her shoulders. Releasing her left hand, Sara brought it above her right, and pulled. She took a step up the side of the boat. Shakily, she repeated the action. By the time she had done all of that three times, the trembling in her arms had become an earthquake and her whole body was shaking.

Above her, the laughing had stopped and sailors were reaching down, trying to grab her. 'Hold on,' she told herself. 'Hold on!' But she couldn't; her feet slipped off the bottom knot and with a scream, she tumbled back into the rowing boat, twisting as she fell and landing heavily. A sharp pain shot through her leg. Looking down she saw a deep cut – dark red and oozing blood. Suddenly, two strong hands grabbed her shoulders. Without a word, the boatman stood her up, tied the rope around her stomach and shouted to his friends. A second later, Sara was hoisted into the air like a bag of rice and hauled up the side.

As soon as she had landed on the deck, she was untied, and one of the sailors – a small man with tiny hands and a nose like a bird – applied a poultice to her leg.

'Don't worry,' said the captain, slapping Sara on the back and grinning, 'it's really just a scratch. You'll be fine.'

The poultice seemed to stop the bleeding, and though her leg still throbbed, and the wound was still raw, Sara was grateful.

'So how does your leg feel, Little Pebble?' asked the captain.

Sara shrugged. 'It still hurts a bit.'

'Well, what do you expect? Xiao Que isn't the Imperial doctor, you know! But if it still hurts when we get back, you can go see Zhao Taicheng.'

'Zhao Taicheng?'

'He *is* the Imperial doctor!'

Sara nodded.

They sat on the wooden deck of the ship, the captain resting his back against the ship's mast. Above them, a single sail billowed in the wind, and around them the other sailors – though they had been told to get back to work by the captain – were paying scant attention to their duties and were instead watching Sara and the captain with enormous interest. Sara would normally have been very embarrassed with all this attention, but she barely noticed the men. She marshalled her thoughts; she still had the saddlebag, and she still needed to find the silk merchant in Bianjing.

The captain continued. 'So why are you so keen to come with us? Why did you run the risk of drowning just to sail to Luoyang?' he asked.

'Where?' Sara asked.

'Luoyang,' said the captain. 'We'll take our cargo of hemp there and bring back Buddhist carvings. My master, Kwong Ming, is a big merchant, you know. And very devout. He owns many ships, many camels, many horses.'

'Luoyang… Is that near Bianjing?' Sara asked.

The captain snorted and gave her a puzzled look. 'Eh… maybe the Imperial doctor needs to examine your head too?'

'What do you mean?' asked Sara.

'We are approaching Bianjing now,' replied the captain. 'Luoyang is hundreds of *li* from Bianjing!'

'What?' Sara yelled. 'I have to go to Bianjing.'

'Well, you can't. We don't have time to stop on the way,' replied the captain.

'But—'

'Captain,' yelled one of the crew, his trembling hand pointing to something up ahead.

The captain leaped to his feet. 'You idiots!' he screamed. 'Bring down the mast! Bring down the mast!'

Sara stood and stared. Looming up ahead, a giant wooden bridge arched over the river. The Rainbow Bridge! It was bustling with people who crowded the stalls lining the bridge's span. One person stood out to her – an old man wearing a bright red kerchief on his head selling small cakes by the dozen – but there were hundreds of people there; people buying, people selling, people leaning over the edge and peering at the boats passing underneath them. As Sara watched and as the boat slowly approached, more of them stopped what they were doing and looked in her direction. Some were pointing. More people joined them. Now they were shouting. Wait a minute…

'Of course!' she said, remembering the scroll. 'The ship's about to get stuck under the bridge!'

'What are you doing?' someone cried from the quayside.

'You are getting too close to the bridge,' cried another.

'Grab hold of this line,' yelled a third, casting a rope in the ship's direction. 'Hurry, before you crash!'

But it was too late. The bridge came rushing towards them and a moment later there was a crash and the horrible crunch and squeal of wood pressed hard against wood. Sailors who were not holding on to the sides were catapulted onto the deck.

Everyone was panicking. People were throwing ropes to the ship and the sailors were dashing about catching the ropes and securing them to the ship. A thought burned in Sara. It could be her way off the ship…

The mast! She could climb it, hang on to the wooden timbers under the bridge, hope that someone pulled her onto the bridge. She gazed up – and up and up the tall mast… *Stupid idea! There must be another way to get off this ship. Think!*

The ship had begun to turn, pulled by the huge crowd of people on the quayside. She stared at the taut ropes lashed to the ship and the long lines of people on the shore heaving on them, straining to pull the ship to the safety of the quayside while the tumbling brown river rushed past. She could wait and hope the ship was pulled away from the bridge towards the safety of the shore, but how long would that take?

She snatched up a short, greasy-looking piece of rope from the deck and, before anyone could stop her, folded it over one of the ropes that the crowd had thrown up to the ship and was pulling on. Holding tightly to either end of the short rope and making sure the saddlebag was securely over her shoulder, she launched herself off the ship. She wasn't sure if friction would stop her movement, but the main rope seemed well greased and she flew, gravity propelling her towards the riverbank.

Sara let go of the short rope a fraction of a second too late.

# CHAPTER 20

—

Feet first, she crashed into the three men leading a group of twelve or more people who were dragging the ship away from the bridge. She knocked them down like ninepins. There were loud protests and shoves. Ignoring the men and the throbbing in her leg, she was congratulating herself for her quick thinking when she froze, eyes fixed on the near distance.

Seven riders, lashing their horses and spewing dust clouds behind them, were hurtling along the riverside towards the stricken ship.

'Hey!', 'Look out!' and 'What are you doing?' the men called, but Sara was determined to put at least a million miles between her and the Gang of the White Fawn.

Hobbling, she dodged her way through the riverbank crowds and scuttled into the first alleyway she found. As soon as she entered the narrow street, she was caught up in a swarm of people. Crammed between wooden buildings, the wave swept her through a chaotic maze of alleyways like a beach ball. Around her, people were bartering, complaining, calling out to their friends and pushing and shoving.

Sara bobbed along. One minute the sun would peek over the wooden buildings and shine in her eyes; the next, it would disappear. She had no idea where she was going, but that didn't matter – if she had no idea where she was, neither would the gang! Clutching the saddlebag to her side, she tried to fight the panic rising in her. She was tired, and her leg was really hurting. In fact, it was *really* throbbing.

Just when she thought she would have to sit down and be trampled by the hordes of people around her, the alley ended and, like a tiny stream emptying into a river, she found herself on a wide, dusty road separating long lines of shops and businesses. There were oxen carts, donkeys, horses and even camels, and there were sedan chairs hurtling along, transported by the fast-moving legs of their human carriers. It was a relief to be on a wider street away from the crush, but if Mo Zei came along this road, she'd be very easy to spot.

She hobbled on, passing building upon building. Most were small, but one had a towering wooden facade and cascading roof. Sniffing the air – onions – she squinted at the sign above the building's doorway: *Sun Yang's Restaurant.* It took her a split second, but, like her instinctively speaking Mandarin, she easily figured out the traditional character for 'restaurant'. Just as she did so her stomach made a sound like rolling thunder. She thought she already knew the answer but nonetheless she checked her pockets. As she suspected – nothing. Her pockets were as empty as her stomach. She kept on walking. A flock of thoughts crowded her brain. How could she find somewhere safe in Bianjing? How could she get the saddlebag to Wan Yi? How could she get someone to look at her leg?' She hobbled past the restaurant. One thing she was sure about: she couldn't just wander around hoping something would turn up. She needed to think. She needed to take control of the situation.

'What I need,' she told herself, 'is a *plan*.'

Grimacing, she continued walking, the saddlebag slapping against her back as she went. Soon, she would have to find somewhere to sit and rest for a little while. As she adjusted the saddlebag, which had slipped from her shoulder, a thought struck her. *What exactly am I carrying? The saddlebag isn't heavy and whatever is in it isn't bulky... And Zhang Guolao didn't tell me not to look inside!*

A short distance away, she saw the tree. Gnarly and tall, it rose outside a building called Lord Wang's Inn. When she reached the tree, she stood for a moment under its shade, eyes closed, enjoying its coolness. She dropped the saddlebag at her feet. The man to her left – skinny, half Sara's size, with lanky, greasy hair – turned and looked at her. He was selling rope from his bamboo cart and arguing about prices with a man wearing a hat like a sombrero. He glared, giving her a look that said, 'Get lost, filthy urchin!'

Sara ignored him and plopped herself beside the saddlebag, shooting back a look that said, 'What you going to do about it?'

They stared at one another. The man's customer was still shouting about the price. The rope seller blinked and turned back to rejoin the argument. *One-nil to me,* Sara thought.

Reaching down, she grabbed the saddlebag's buckle. 'I've got a right to know what I'm carrying!' she told herself as she unfastened the latch. She peered inside.

For a moment, she was speechless. 'What the…?' she said, grabbing the scrunched-up ball of brightly coloured material tucked away in the corner and pulling it out. She stared at it. Un-be-lie-va-ble! All this fuss over… *this*? She held up the piece of perfectly square red, green and yellow fabric about the size of a large hand-kerchief. It was decorated with jagged, swirling patterns, was cool to the touch and quite heavy. Silk, perhaps, but not like any she had seen before – it had an unusual stiffness, almost like it had been starched a little or was made of thicker than normal silk strands.

She peered more closely at the design and realised she was looking at dragons. Tails, fierce faces, claws and serpentine bodies wound their way up and down and across the fabric. Best of all, between the dragons' bodies, there were little jade-coloured circles: puzzle balls. The maker of the piece of silk had done an incredible job because the puzzle balls were practically three-dimensional. On each of their outer surfaces, as though carved in stone, there were more dragons. But there were inner surfaces too, and more dragons on each of them, the surfaces and the dragons growing smaller and smaller as they progressed towards the centre of each of the puzzle balls.

'Dragons within dragons,' Sara whispered. It *was* really beautiful, but what was so important about it? And why did Mo Zei and the Gang of the White Fawn want it so badly? Why did Wan Yi?

She stuffed the piece of silk back into the saddlebag. She looked up – and gaped at the sight before her.

# CHAPTER 21

—

Here was a caravan on the famous Silk Road! From where she sat, she thought it didn't look nearly as glamorous as the wonders she'd imagined. The caravans in picture books she'd read as a kid all looked so cheerful, elegant and colourful. Here, though, everyone looked exhausted, especially the animals that were carrying heavy packs lashed to their backs. Most of them were donkeys and horses, but a few were camels, which she'd never seen close up before. Such long legs and huge, broad hooves. And look at the height of their riders! Perched between the two humps, wobbling from side to side and towering above her, they reminded her of acrobats on a high wire. What were the two-humped camels called again – bactrian? Sara shook her head. Lily would know.

Lily…

She and Joaquin and all the rest of her class. What was happening while she was here? Was her body still in the Beijing Palace Museum? Was she still alive in the real world? The real world! What exactly was that? The cut on her leg felt very real. So did the dusty air she was breathing and the saddlebag she was sitting on.

'Focus,' she told herself. She had to think about how to find this woman, Wan Yi. First, what did she know about her? Answer: almost nothing – except she was a silk merchant. Hmm. Were there many female silk merchants? She hadn't seen many women so far, apart from fleeting glimpses of them in sedans and a few on horseback with veiled travelling hats and servants on foot in front of the horse to clear

a path through the crowds. So maybe Wan Yi was quite unusual…
If she was unusual, lots of people might know her, which could help.
Okay, what else? Wan Yi was a silk merchant. So… so maybe some of
the traders in the caravan knew her? She looked at the hard, weath-
er-beaten faces of the men trudging past, eyes cast to the ground
or else staring mindlessly at the road in front of them. Could she
imagine any of them wanting to stop and help? Not really, no. Okay,
who else? How about someone who *sells* silk? Like a dress shop? Or…

She gave a derisive laugh as she looked up. Word of the day?
Serendipity!

Snatching up the saddlebag, she painfully rose to her feet and
hobbled across the street to where Jinan Lui's Fine Needle Shop sat
– a lonely-looking, slender building separate from the others.

'Hello?' Sara said, standing at the doorway. 'Anybody here?'
She stood, hardly breathing, waiting. No answer. She called again.
Still no answer. The interior of the shop was about the size of her
bedroom and badly lit; the sun did not reach inside and the shade
from the trees outside made it even darker.

Slowly, Sara's eyes adjusted. It was a Chinese Aladdin's cave! On
all four walls, bolts of silk, one on top of the other in a thousand
different patterns, climbed all the way to the ceiling. The smell of
cloth – lots and lots of cloth, slightly sour, along with the tang of
smoke from two smouldering incense sticks – filled the air. There
were three counters in front of her – one long, the other two shorter.
All three had glass countertops and below them were boxes and
boxes of stuff. She inched forward. Peering into the boxes, she saw
they were full of needles: long ones, shiny ones, tiny ones, huge ones.

'Oh!' she cried. She jumped, startled, as part of the wall swung
open and a man carrying bolts of silk stepped out of a hidden door.
Head down, he was humming a tune.

The man looked up sharply, as though suddenly sensing Sara,
and their eyes met. His calmness evaporated in an instant.

# CHAPTER 22

'What are you doing in here? Get out of my shop, you filthy urchin! Out! Out!' he barked, throwing down the bolts of silk and pointing to the door as he came around the counter.

Sara had had enough. 'I'M NOT AN URCHIN!' she yelled, so loudly she surprised herself.

The man froze for a second. But only a second. 'What have you stolen from me? There is no money in here. Leave, I tell you. Leave!' He reached out to grab Sara, but she weaved away.

'Okay! Okay! I'm going!' she said. 'Take it easy.'

This was a waste of time. She'd find some other silk seller instead. But as she turned, she glanced at the counter. The bolt of silk at the top of the pile was of similar colours and pattern, though definitely not as beautiful…

'Wait!' she cried, extending one arm and frantically digging into the saddlebag with the other. 'Look!' She held up the piece of silk from Zhang Guolao. 'Look! It's similar to the one you have! I just want to ask *one* question… Please.'

With his flat hair, small pointy ears, and eyebrows raised like bird wings, the man looked like a little pixie. Although he was surrounded by sumptuous silk, his own clothes were tatty, the collar and sleeves of the robe he wore both frayed and grubby. He opened his mouth, but instead of issuing angry words, it hung loose. His eyes had locked on to what Sara was holding, watching it like a hawk eyeing a rabbit.

'Where did you get that?' he asked and reached out.

Sara pulled the piece of silk away and took a step backwards. 'I didn't steal it, if that's what you mean. It was given to me. I've got to take it to someone called Wan Yi. I came in here because she's a silk merchant and you sell silk. Do you know her?'

'May I?' the man asked, reaching out again.

'If you give it back,' Sara said, holding the silk close.

The man nodded.

'I'm trusting you,' Sara reminded him.

'Yes, yes!' he hissed.

A little reluctantly, Sara dropped it into his outstretched palms.

Like a father looking at a newly born baby, the man pored over every centimetre of the fabric. 'It is… exquisite!' he whispered.

'Do you mind?' she said, holding out a hand. 'I'd like it back.'

'How much you want for it?'

Sara noticed he had gripped it tightly in his fist. 'I don't want anything. It's not for sale,' she said firmly.

The little man's eyes suddenly narrowed and Sara had a nasty feeling he was thinking about keeping it.

'I'd like it back *now*. It's not *yours*. It's *mine*.'

The man continued to stare hard at her. His greedy, eager expression frightened her a little. Then he pursed his lips and slowly released them. His whole face lost its tautness and his seagull eyebrows, which had sunk low, rose higher. 'So,' he said, dropping the silk into her hands and turning away quickly, 'you want information?'

Relieved, Sara pushed the silk into the saddlebag and closed it. 'Yes, I need to find Wan Yi. Do you know her?'

'Why do you want to see her?'

Sara noticed he had avoided answering her question yet again. 'I was told she was the wisest person in the city. Do you know where I can find her?'

'Maybe.'

'Okay. So, where?'

The man picked up a bolt of silk on the counter and gazed at it. 'Give a man a fish,' he said, still gazing at the bolt, 'and you feed him for a day. Teach a man to fish, and you feed him for a lifetime.'

Sara puffed up her cheeks and blew noisily. Did everyone in this place talk in riddles? 'Sorry, you've lost me.'

'Look around you. What is missing?'

Sara looked. 'Er…'

'Customers!' the man cried, slamming down the bolt. 'Where are all the customers? Look at all the beautiful silk I have!' He pointed to the walls. 'Look at all the needles I sell!' He pointed to the counters. 'Where are the people to buy my goods? Where?'

Sara had no idea where.

'I can take your money—'

*What money?* thought Sara. *I don't have any!*

'—but it will only feed me for a day. I need someone to teach me how to get customers. Otherwise my business is doomed.' When he said 'doomed' he slumped onto the counter and covered his eyes. From the rise and fall of his shoulders Sara could tell he was sobbing.

Embarrassed, she wondered what to do. Maybe she should leave. If one silk seller knew Wan Yi, then others might too. Surely she could find another one. The man blubbered loudly. Even if she wanted to help him, what did she know about selling silk? Nothing! She scratched her head. It did seem a shame just to leave… If this were 21st-century China, what would companies do to attract more customers? Of course!

'Are you Jinan Lui?' Sara asked.

Without looking up, the man nodded.

'And it's your shop?'

He nodded again.

'You should make an advert,' Sara said. 'Advertise your shop.'

Jinan Lui snivelled and wiped his nose on his sleeve. 'What?' he asked, his red eyes gazing at her.

'Businesses advertise,' Sara said. 'When they want more customers, they advertise.'

'I don't understand. What is "advertise"?'

'You make a poster or… or a flyer. Tell people about your shop and why they should come to it. Tell them it's the best shop in the city, that they won't get a better deal on silk anywhere else – stuff like that.'

Jinan Lui's brows creased. 'But they can get better deals elsewhere. Mine is not the cheapest silk. There are plenty of—'

'Then two for one!'

'What?'

'Two for one! Buy one and get one free. Customers buy one piece of silk and get another piece free. Even when you stop offering the two-for-one deal, they'll still keep coming because they associate your shop with good deals!'

Jinan Lui's eyes shone. 'So I advertise my shop? Make a paper telling people about the deal?'

Sara nodded. 'You've got it!'

'And will people come?'

'What other ideas do you have?'

Jinan Lui nodded. 'True. I have none.' A smile spread across his face. 'Can you help me make it?'

'The advert?'

'Yes.'

'If you'll tell me where I can find Wan Yi.'

Jinan Lui looked down. 'I have a confession to make,' he said quietly.

Sara frowned. 'Okaaay…'

'I don't know where she is.'

'But you told me you knew her!'

'I do! I have heard her name before, but I don't know where you can find her.' He looked up and smiled. 'But,' he cried, lifting a finger in front of his face, 'I do know the name of a woman who can help you. She is the most famous fortune teller in Bianjing.'

'And how's that going to help me find Wan Yi?' Sara asked angrily.

'How will it not? She is a fortune teller. If anyone can help, she can!'

Sara folded her arms.

'Will you help me?'

This wasn't part of the plan.

'Please?' Jinan Lui said.

Sara gave a long sigh. 'Get me a piece of paper,' she said a little waspishly, her leg still throbbing and hot. 'We'll need to design it first.'

# CHAPTER 23

—

Outside, after spending more than an hour in the silk shop, Sara felt hotter than ever. As she shuffled along, she thought about the advert she had made for Jinan Lui. It was just a simple design on a piece of paper – his shop name on top and its location on the bottom. He would need to have the design engraved on a copper plate. Then it could be hand printed and distributed. Jinan Lui had decided to have 500 copies made and post them all over the city. In the end, the two-for-one deal hadn't been added. 'Let them come and discover it!' he had said. Fair enough. Just to make the advert a bit more appealing, Sara had added the picture of a rabbit. 'It's your logo,' she had told him, which she immediately regretted because she had to then spend the next ten minutes explaining what a logo was. But the important thing was Jinan Lui had kept his promise and told her where to find Madam Zhong, the fortune teller.

Sara hurried along the street and turned left into a narrow alley. 'Look out!' someone shouted as a sedan hurtled towards her.

Sara jumped back, pressing her body against the wooden shacks that lined the alley, just in time to dodge the sedan and a kick from one of the sedan carriers.

She peeled herself off the wooden shack. The sedan carriers disappeared in a cloud of dust. Sara wiped her eyes and gawped: halfway up the deserted alleyway was the smallest, most crooked and ancient-looking house she'd ever seen in her life. And carved into its wooden door was a shape – of three hares, each sharing an ear so that a triangle was formed at the centre and a circle was formed around it by their bodies. Not only that, the carving was alive! Each of the hares was running in slow motion, bounding across an invisible field, their legs turning and turning and turning, though their bodies remained in the same place.

Sara read the name on the door. *Madam Zhong.*

Sara's head felt as light as a mote of dust. She reached towards the hares. But as her fingertips came within touching distance of them, when all she needed to do was straighten her arm just a little, the door gently swung away from her. She stepped back. Half in sunlight and half in shadow, the door looked like an invitation to enter – or a warning to leave. She held her breath. Moments passed. Nothing happened. She breathed out. She peered into the shack's dark interior. Was there something glowing in there? She glanced back down the little alleyway, then at the door. The hares were gone! By this stage, nothing was going to surprise her. What should she do? Was she meant to go in? She bit her lip. If it brought her closer to finding Wan Yi, she had to go in…

Stepping forward, she tried to edge past the door and enter the shack as quietly as she could. Fail! The ancient floorboards beneath her feet immediately cried out like furious cats. She cringed but kept going. It was unbelievably dark, but was there something in front of her? She moved towards it, sniffing the air as she went – wood smoke, aromatic logs, dried flowers. She moved closer to the yellow glow, which flickered and danced in front of her. Now she could see that the light was actually three separate lights. Candles! They were candles, but they were floating in mid-air. It took her another second to realise that the candles were in fact on a table.

'Hmm! About time!' said a croaky voice. 'Are you going to stand there like a heron looking for lunch, or are you going to sit down?'

Sara froze. 'Hello?'

There was the sound of rustling fabric and creaking wood. 'Yes! Hello, my lovely! Nice to meet you!'

A moment later, more flickering yellow light spread as eight or nine additional candles were lit and the door slammed shut with a bang.

Sara gave a yelp of surprise.

'Oh, behave yourself!' said an old woman. She was sitting at the table, watching Sara through hooded eyes. She curled her forefinger and beckoned Sara forward. The old woman's cheeks, which were round and deeply wrinkled, rose and her face broke into a toothless smile.

For a second, Sara thought about turning around and running out of there. But the old woman seemed to read her mind. 'I don't bite, you know! Now, sit!' she said.

Sara hesitated, then limped across the small room and sat on a stool at the table. She stared at the woman. She had the biggest ears Sara had ever seen. They seemed to start at the top of her head and reach past her jaw.

'My name,' said the old woman, suddenly raising her voice so that it sounded a hundred times stronger than her body looked capable of producing, 'is Madam Zhong, and I am the most famous fortune teller in all China. You've probably heard of me...'

Sara raised her eyebrows. *Not until an hour ago,* she thought, but said nothing.

Madam Zhong shrugged. 'I am the blessed one. Dark learning I have studied; the ten thousand things I know. Through me, the celestial wind blows and I play its tune... Would you like a cup of tea?'

Sara licked her dry lips, but before she could answer, Madam Zhong was off again.

'I have travelled in spirit. I know Mount Kunlun and I know the Earth's navel! Speak, child,' Madam Zhong commanded. 'Say more. From your voice, I shall know from where you have come.'

*Good luck with that,* thought Sara. 'What would you like to know?'

'Well, let's start with your age,' said Madam Zhong.

'I'm 14,' Sara said.

'Ah, you were born in the Year of the Rabbit, yes?'

Sara nodded.

Madam Zhong clapped her hands and the candles flickered furiously. 'I can always tell. Rabbits are calm and unassuming; peacemakers, in fact.' She smiled. 'You are sensitive to the needs of people around you and do little things thoughtfully to make them happy, yes?'

Sara thought of Granny Tang with a pang of guilt. 'Well, I try to be, but sometimes...'

'Yes, yes, rabbits can be secretive, cunning even,' Madam Zhong interrupted. 'Now think about this – one day you will be an ancestor, a bright river out of which many generations will have flown.'

'Okay. Good,' Sara replied, wondering how rude it would be if she just got up and left.

Madam Zhong continued. 'Now... You are from Kashgar, yes?'

'No. Actually, I'm from Beijing.'

Madam Zhong shrugged and lit three more candles. When she was finished, she sniffed and said, 'Never heard of it. It's far away, yes?'

'You could say that,' Sara said, thinking, *Yes, about 800 years away.*

'So,' said Madam Zhong, straightening her back, 'what is your question?'

'Question? What question?'

'Your question,' said Madam Zhong. 'You must have a question. Unless you have a question, I can't give you an answer.'

Sara frowned. 'I suppose that makes sense.' She paused, thinking, then opened her mouth again.

'Don't tell me your question!' Madam Zhong cried. 'Just keep it in your head.'

Sara nodded. There were so many questions, but the main one was where she could find Wan Yi.

'Are you ready to begin?'

Sara nodded again.

'So let us begin!'

# Chapter 24

Eyes flashing, Madam Zhong cried, 'Look!' She opened her hands and cast the objects in them across the table.

Sara looked. Scattered across the table, there were about fifty little sticks, all of them lying higgledy-piggledy. Madam Zhong ran her eyes over the sticks again and again; then she turned her shining face towards Sara.

'Um. Nice sticks...' It was all Sara could think of saying.

'Yarrow sticks. They will answer your question,' said Madam Zhong. 'Gather them up.'

Sara did as she was instructed. Madam Zhong plucked one from the pile in Sara's hand. 'Don't touch that one,' she said, laying it on the table. Sara nodded.

Madam Zhong gave her lots of instructions: take this stick, take that stick, lay this stick on top of another stick. Finally, Madam Zhong said, 'Now lay all the remaining sticks in your hand across the stick that I took out at the start.' Sara laid down nine sticks. 'Old yin,' Madam Zhong mumbled. She peered at Sara. 'Well?' she said.

'Well, what?' asked Sara.

'Well, what are you waiting for?' said Madam Zhong.

'I don't know what to do!'

Madam Zhong shook her head. 'Gather all the sticks again, take out one, divide the sticks into two bundles, and repeat the process...' she said slowly as though she were talking to a child.

Sara felt a bit cross, but she had to have an answer to her question, so she repeated the process and this time she laid down eight sticks.

'Old yang,' said Madam Zhong. 'Do it again!'

Sara sighed and did the whole thing again… and again… and again and again.

Finally, Madam Zhong held up a hand. 'That's enough,' she said, flicking through the book next to her. 'Ah!' she exclaimed, turning to a page near the front of the book and pointing at a shape with six lines in it. 'The Army is your lower trigram and Holding Together is the upper! Very interesting. So… what do you think of the answer to your question?'

'What do you mean?' Sara said, trying hard not to sound very, *very* frustrated. 'What answer? I didn't get one!'

Madam Zhong looked aghast. 'Well, I think you did!'

'Look,' Sara said, 'someone told me Wan Yi could help me, if I delivered something to her. She's supposed to be the smartest person in—'

'Never heard of her!' cried Madam Zhong, throwing up her arms. 'Now pay attention and let me explain! An army needs good order, discipline, if you like. It must have a common objective to unite its warriors. The good general knows when to push forward, when to pull back…'

'How is this helping me find Wan Yi?' asked Sara. 'I'm not a general and I don't have an army!'

Madam Zhong appeared not to hear her. 'You have great power,' she continued, 'but your power is like a river that flows deep underground. You must work to access this power. Great effort will be required. But your potential is mighty: water changes mountains – and many mountains await you.' Madam Zhong stood up. 'I think it is time for you to see to your leg. Doesn't it hurt?'

'Yes, it does,' replied Sara, amazed. 'But how did you know? Was it the sticks? Did they tell you?'

'Don't be silly!' scoffed Madam Zhong. 'You were limping when you walked to the table.'

'Oh,' said Sara.

'The sticks have spoken,' said Madam Zhong, slamming shut the book she had been consulting. 'Now it is time for you to see the Imperial doctor.'

'But I have to find Wan Yi first. I have to give her the saddlebag. I promised Zhang Guo—'

'Be quiet, child!' snapped Madam Zhong. 'Were you not listening? A good general knows when to push forward and when to retreat. First, seek the doctor to treat your leg – consolidate your position – then push forward towards your objective, which is finding Wan Yi, whoever she is. Now, would you like that cup of tea?'

But before Sara could answer, Madam Zhong came around the table. Reaching up, she put a hand on Sara's shoulder and steered Sara towards the door. The old woman's grip was surprisingly strong and Sara wasn't going to argue with her, even if she did look like a gust of wind would knock her over. 'Come again, dear girl,' said Madam Zhong. 'Shame about the tea. We'll have it next time, yes?'

Sara nodded, then said, 'Wait! I can't go to the Imperial doctor. I don't have any money.'

'Money?' said Madam Zhong. 'Well, if you had something to sell, I might be able to help you. What about that saddlebag you are holding on to? Is there something in it, I wonder?'

Sara tightened her grip on it.

'I would pay well for something nice,' said Madam Zhong. 'You would have enough to buy nice clothes, good food, a sedan chair…'

'No. I'm sorry, but it's not mine to sell,' she replied, thinking that even if she could sell it, the piece of fabric wouldn't be worth much.

Madam Zhong looked at her long and hard. 'Well, that is a pity,' she said. 'You might be lucky – sometimes the doctor treats filthy urchins like you for free. But be careful! Make sure you still have two kidneys when you leave!' Madam Zhong's eyes disappeared behind her wrinkly cheeks as she gave a dry, wheezing laugh that shook her whole body.

*Very funny,* thought Sara. *And if someone calls me a filthy urchin again I'm going to scream.* Another thought occurred to her. 'Er… I also don't have any money to pay you.'

Madam Zhong stopped laughing and wiped her eyes. 'Well, of course you don't, I know that! I'm a fortune teller, remember?'

# CHAPTER 25

▬

Sara stepped out of the alley and back on to the busy street. The sunshine felt warm on her back. As she hobbled along the busy thoroughfare, people of all sorts came and went in and out of the shops, tea houses and restaurants stretching in front of her – officials with tall, boxy hats wearing long robes and scarves draped at the waist; soldiers with swords at their sides; workers in short breeches and dull robes tucked into their waistbands.

As she hobbled, she repeated the directions that Madam Zhong had given her to the Imperial doctor's house. The trouble was she was feeling tired and hungry and the more she repeated the directions, the more confused she became. 'Left' became 'right' and 'in front of' became 'behind' until all that remained was gobbledygook. She stopped walking. Despite the sunshine, she felt a cold shiver creep up her spine. A vision of the Gang of the White Fawn – their cruel faces and dead eyes – chilled her blood. She had to get to the doctor's as quickly as possible. Then she had to find Wan Yi.

She looked up and down the road. Nearby, a wheelwright was making a wheel, his hammer thump, thump, thumping... An ox cart trundled past, then another cart, this time with four donkeys pulling it. The dusty animals looked utterly exhausted – even more tired and hungry than she felt. She was wondering if she should go back to Madam Zhong and ask for directions again when a sudden burst of applause caught her attention. Up ahead, a tall man with hair gathered up in a topknot and wearing a jacket with very broad cuffs, was standing under a sign that said, *Storyteller*. In front of him, a gaggle of children stood, cheering. *Perhaps he knows where the Imperial doctor's house is,* thought Sara. As she approached, one of the children dropped a coin into a small, wooden box sitting on the storyteller's stall. The children fell silent as the storyteller began another story.

'Now what story shall I tell you?' the storyteller asked himself. 'Hmm... Ah! I know! Confucius!'

The children nodded, already under his spell.

'Well,' said the storyteller, 'many years after Confucius's death, Confucius's ideas about proper behaviour and the responsibility of leaders to take care of their subjects began spreading across the country. When the first Qin emperor heard about Confucius's ideas, he was furious. "My subjects will get the wrong ideas in their heads," he said. "They'll question my actions. I can't have that!" So the emperor decided to take some of his soldiers to Confucius's grave. He wanted to punish Confucius by *smashing his bones.*'

When he said that, one or two of the children laughed nervously.

The storyteller continued. 'The emperor had Confucius's grave opened, but he was in for a surprise. When he entered the grave, instead of finding Confucius's bones, he found a bed and a table. That's right, a bed and a table! And on the table there was a letter. This is what it said: *You have broken into my grave, you are sitting on my bed, and you are reading my note.* When he read the note, the emperor was furious. Then he saw a rabbit scurry out of the tomb, which he believed was the spirit of Confucius. In his anger, the emperor ordered his soldiers to kill the rabbit. It got away. This did not help the emperor's mood at all. As he stood in the forest, a chill wind rose suddenly. The next day, the emperor came down with a fever and died.'

The children cheered. 'Another!' they cried. 'Tell us another.'

The storyteller was smiling, but he was also shaking his head. 'Pay for the tale!' he kept saying. 'Pay for the tale.'

*Like ancient Chinese TV,* though Sara.

As they ran out of money, one by one, the children gave up trying to persuade him to continue and slowly drifted away. The storyteller looked her up and down. She met his snooty gaze. They stared at one another. The storyteller lowered himself onto the three-legged stool behind him. Sara's eyes found the low-level table next to him. On it, six unbelievably delicious-looking jade-green rice balls lay on a plate.

The storyteller followed her eyes. 'Ahh… *qingtuan*,' he said, leaning over and picking up one of the rice balls. 'Aren't they wonderful?' He popped it into his mouth. 'Of course,' he said, chewing with his mouth open, 'the green reminds us that even while we honour the dead at festival time, we should also celebrate new life.'

In her head, Sara repeated the words 'even while we honour the dead, we should also celebrate new life' sarcastically. *Easy to be philosophical,* she thought, *when your stomach is full.* Once again, *her* stomach rumbled like a train.

The plan was to get to the doctor's house so that she could have her leg attended to and continue her search for Wan Yi more easily. But some fuel to keep her going wouldn't be a bad idea, would it? Problem was, she didn't have any money …But maybe she didn't need it.

'I'll trade you!'

The storyteller eyed her suspiciously. 'What?'

'I am from a far country,' Sara replied. 'A place where movies… I mean, stories… are as abundant as the birds. I'll tell you a story you've *never* heard before and in return, you give me those.' She pointed to the rice balls.

'Go away!'

'Why?' Sara cried. 'My story is worth many, many rice balls. When people hear it, you'll be the most famous storyteller in all of Bianjing.'

Sara could almost see his lips repeating 'the most famous storyteller in Bianjing'.

'How long is it?' he asked.

'Er... 20 minutes?'

His eyes widened just a fraction. 'Two rice balls,' he said after a pause.

Sara shook her head. 'Three! One before and two after!'

He stroked his hairless chin.

Sara's stomach growled again.

'Very well – it's a deal.' He passed her the plate. Sara plucked the biggest rice ball off, gave it a treasured look, and popped it into her mouth. Deep joy and happiness! She just about managed to taste its sweet bean paste before she swallowed it.

'The story?' he said.

'Okay,' Sara said. 'The story.' *Wait till he hears this one!* she thought. 'A long time ago,' she said, relishing the words, 'in a galaxy far—'

'What's a galaxy?'

'A part of space.'

'Space?'

'The heavens! The heavens!' she cried, pointing to the sky.

'Ah,' the storyteller said.

Sara gave him a grumpy look and continued. 'Once, in a galaxy far, far away there was a civil war, and rebel spaceships were—'

'Spaceship? What's a spaceship?'

Sara sighed. This wasn't working. 'Okay, okay,' she said, holding up her hands. Maybe that was a story for another day. 'Just wait a second.' What she needed was something low-tech, easy to grasp.

But what? She gazed around. Shops, people, the stall, the storyteller, herself – a filthy urchin. Filthy urchin! Of course! 'You're going to love this.' The storyteller eyed her – suspiciously, she thought. Smiling, she continued. 'Once upon a time, there was a young, beautiful girl, and her name was Cinderella…'

'Cinderella?'

'Yes, Cinderella.'

The storyteller made a face.

'What now?'

'I don't like the name.'

'So change it! Choose something else!'

The storyteller stroked his chin.

Sara tapped her foot.

'I like Yexian,' he finally said.

'Fine, let's call her Yexian.'

The storyteller nodded and Sara began.

For the next 20 minutes, the storyteller listened while Sara told him about wicked stepmothers, horrible stepsisters, fairy god-mothers, magical mice, elegant shoes, pumpkin coaches, handsome princes, grand ballrooms, eager searches. When she finished – when Yexian had been found and had married the prince – the storyteller was ecstatic.

'Oh, wondrous, wondrous urchin! You are a master teller of tales. A lord weaver of yarns! Stay. Stay and tell me more,' he cried, thrusting the plate of rice balls towards her. 'Take them all and tell me another, I beg you!'

'I can't,' Sara said. 'I have to see the doctor. It's really hurting.' She pointed to her leg.

'Of course, of course! You must take care of yourself. But you will come back, won't you?'

'I… Er…' Sara said.

'Do you have any money?'

Sara shook her head.

'Now is the springtime festival and festivals are times of great generosity. Please take this,' he said, handing her a stack of coins pierced through the middle and threaded on a piece of rope. 'Take them! Take them all!'

In the history of the world, had anyone, Sara wondered, ever enjoyed Cinderella as much as he had? Probably not!

'One final thing,' Sara said, bending her leg back and forth, which had grown even stiffer from standing. 'Could you tell me where I can find the Imperial doctor's house?'

# CHAPTER 26

—

Sara followed the storyteller's directions and within a few minutes arrived at a large square full of people.

'The marketplace,' Sara muttered. The doctor's house wasn't far away. In fact, once she crossed the marketplace, she would almost be there. But Sara couldn't help staring at the sight in front of her. The marketplace was a great sea of languages, colours and smells. Hundreds of people were in the square. Some were buying, some were selling, some were Chinese merchants, some were not.

She was amazed at the variety of clothes – the rough, sturdy weave of the horsemen's coats, the silk that flowed around the women, the great many headdresses, turbans, scarves. So many different styles, so many different cultures! But it was the variety of accents, the singsong and staccato, that amazed her most. It reminded her of the birdhouse at the Beijing Zoo. Everyone was furiously bargaining – pushing prices up and haggling them down – all at once! She had never heard so much scoffing, promising, cajoling and laughing.

She stepped into the storm of noise and action, weaving her way between the saddle blankets laid out on the ground and the carts and tables. She dodged the men striding towards their next business deal, nipped between stalls covered with black and red lacquer ware, scooted past dozing horses and camels brought to their knees as their jaws ground crookedly. All the while, the tang of cardamom, the sweet fragrance of sandalwood and a hundred other spices and smells swam in the air.

Sara paused beside a woman selling baskets made of woven reeds. The baskets were covered with small yellow and blue flowers, made from interlocking fibres. The woman was sitting on the ground, dyed reeds spread out on a blanket next to her, and threading another strand into the large pattern she was working. Sara admired the woman's nimble hands, which moved rhythmically back and forth. Another flower emerged. The woman looked up, smiled, and said something that Sara didn't understand.

She needed to get to the doctor's house as soon as possible so that she could continue the search for Wan Yi, but she was in awe; goods that had travelled thousands of miles along an ancient route that stretched all the way from China to Rome were being sold here. The traders selling the goods would have fought their way across the Karakum Desert, the Mountains of Heaven and Hindu Kush, surviving drought, starvation and bandits. It was amazing, really amazing!

Then it happened. As though a cold, slimy slug was creeping up her spine, Sara felt a chill that made the hairs on her arms stand on end. Whatever was causing it was behind her. Slowly, very slowly, she turned her head. A few steps away, a gem merchant dressed in flowing silk robes stood behind a small table covered with dark green silk on which a silver set of scales stood next to lapis lazuli gemstones. He was facing Sara, but in front of him, with his back to Sara, was a large, bulky man with wild hair, wearing the blue cloak of the Gang of the White Fawn. He and the gem merchant were in the middle of an argument.

'I told you,' shouted the gem merchant, 'I don't know what you're talking about! No one has tried to sell any jade to me!' There was a growl, but Sara couldn't make out what had been said. 'No! I haven't seen a girl. Why are you asking all these stupid questions? Why don't you just—' continued the merchant, but he didn't get a chance to finish his sentence. Instead, the other man's huge arms shot forward and his two meaty hands shoved the merchant in the chest. One second the merchant was standing; the next, his feet were in the air and he was flying backwards. *CRASH!* The merchant landed in a heap amongst a hundred pots and pans, which sent the seller of the pots and pans – a wrinkled old woman who looked at least a hundred years old – into a rage. Grabbing a pan, she fixed a claw onto the merchant's collar and began beating him while a crowd, eager for free entertainment, formed a circle around them and began laughing and jeering.

Sara crouched behind a camel, watching as the large man in the blue cloak drew his sword and marched towards the fallen merchant. The poor merchant, whacked mercilessly by the old woman, watched in horror as the man approached. Desperately, he tried to free himself from the pots-and-pans seller, which only enraged her more.

Suddenly Mo Zei – in his long, black cloak – glided into the circle formed by onlookers and grabbed the hulking man by the shoulder. He swirled around, his sword raised, his face twisted in anger. But as soon as he saw who was holding his shoulder, the man's expression changed and he cast his eyes down at his feet.

Mo Zei turned to the crowd, his narrow face breaking into a smile. He raised his pointed chin, ready to address everyone. Sara shrunk even lower until only her eyebrows and the very top of her head were peeping out from behind the camel.

'I am sorry, my friends,' Mo Zei said. 'It was just a slight misunderstanding, that's all. Nothing to worry about. Everything is being taken care of. We apologise for upsetting anyone.' He gave the pots-and-pans seller a bow.

'Bah!' the old woman replied, muttering about respect and decency as she released the merchant, who scurried away. The crowd laughed and the large man in the blue cloak grunted and sheathed his sword. There was a brief lull, then the other merchants, eager to sell their wares, began calling loudly. The crowd, seeing that the fun was over, started to drift away.

While the two men from the Gang of the White Fawn had their backs turned to her, Sara crept away and sneaked out of the square.

# CHAPTER 27

The sign above the door said, *Zhao Taicheng – Imperial Doctor.*

*At last,* thought Sara. She stepped towards the door, and was about to knock but stopped. Something had made her glance backwards. She looked along the street. There was no sign of Mo Zei or his large friend. Good. But *something* wasn't right. What was the matter? She shivered. It felt as though she was being watched, that someone, or something, was tracing her footsteps, following her like a shadow. She stepped into the doorway, swivelled around, and peeked into the street. Horses were trotting past, sedan carriers were waiting for customers, restaurant patrons were eating and laughing, and the afternoon sun was sinking gradually towards the west. With her heart beating as fast as a bird's, Sara scanned every face in the street, but no one was paying her any attention. After a few moments more, she faced the door and knocked. When there was no reply, she pushed open the heavy, wooden door and stepped inside.

Sara found herself in a small, square room – the waiting room, she guessed. A door to another room faced her. Along the wall on her left, there was a wooden bench; opposite the wooden bench, a long landscape painting hung on the wall. The painting showed two mountains wrapped in mist.

Sara sat on the bench and laid the saddlebag at her feet. Now that she was seated and still, she could feel her leg throbbing painfully. As she rubbed it, she heard a man's voice.

'No, I haven't heard anything from the court astronomer. Nor has there been any news from Su Song's astronomical clock tower. If there were to be an eclipse, I am sure we would have been informed.'

Another voice, a woman's, asked a muffled question. The man answered again. 'That I cannot predict. May I suggest you speak to Madam Zhong?'

Sara snorted. *Madam Zhong! If you like tea, you'd better have some before you go!*

The voices came closer. The man was talking. 'My pleasure. But please remember to take the potion after you eat.' Then the door to the other room opened and in came a woman followed by a man in a long, dark silk robe which reached to the ground and covered most of his black slippers. Sara stood. The woman thanked the doctor again. She turned and Sara bowed. The woman had a kind face, moon-shaped and pale with delicately curved, almond eyes that gazed steadily at Sara. She was taller than many of the men Sara had seen, and her hair – dark and lustrous and swept into a magnificent crest – made her seem even taller. The silk gown she wore was cut low at the neck, covered in radiantly red flowers and flowing to the ground. Across her shoulders and forearms, a diaphanous silk scarf was draped, so thin and delicate it barely touched her skin.

'What are you doing in here?' the doctor cried, the two strands of his drooping moustache twitching like agitated worms.

'I've hurt my leg,' said Sara, rubbing the wound. 'I need treatment.'

'I am the Imperial doctor,' he roared. 'I do not treat filthy—'

'Doctor Zhao?' The woman's voice was soft yet impossible to ignore.

'Yes, madam?' the doctor asked.

'It would be a personal favour to me if you would attend to this young lady. Is that possible?'

'Of course it is, madam!' the doctor cried. 'I would be happy to.'

The woman closed her eyes softly in acknowledgement. 'Please charge the cost to my account.'

Sara smiled at the woman. 'Thank you.'

With a tilt of the head, the woman returned Sara's smile, and with her fragrance following her – jasmine? – she left.

As soon as the door was closed, the doctor's smile vanished. 'What's the problem?' he asked curtly.

Sara pulled up the leg of her breeches.

'I see,' said Doctor Zhao, making a pyramid with his fingers. He fixed his eyes on Sara's face and, for a few uncomfortable moments, Sara felt like she was a bug under a microscope. The doctor frowned and motioned with his palm towards the consultation room door. 'In there,' he said.

Sara limped past him and entered a small, brightly lit room with high windows on one wall.

'Sit!' said the doctor.

Sara sat down on a chair next to a low table and glanced around. There was a deep sink below the windows. In one corner, a kettle hung over a small fire. Next to her, there was a long cupboard with hundreds of small drawers. The doctor had turned his back to her and was busy with something. To her right, beyond the low table, there were several wooden and iron chests, and beyond them, a wooden bed.

Suddenly, the doctor turned around. Sara gasped. In the doctor's hand was a murderously sharp knife. Before Sara could say or do anything, the doctor stepped past her and went to the cupboard. Sara took a deep breath and let it out slowly. 'Relax!' she told herself. She turned and watched the doctor as he began sliding open the little wooden drawers in the cupboard and pulling out handfuls of dark and twisted things – they looked like dried plants, but Sara wasn't sure. Using the knife to cut pieces from each of the things, the doctor dropped the pieces in a mortar, and returned the remainder to the drawers.

When he had finished taking things from the cupboard, he picked up two different-sized gourds and sprinkled some of their contents into the mortar too. When all of that was done, he snatched up a stone pestle and pounded the contents of the mortar. After a few moments, he added the ground powder to a bowl and poured in a dash of hot water from the kettle. Then he mixed everything thoroughly, emptied the mixture into another bowl in which thin gauze had already been placed, gathered the ends of the gauze and tied them together. While he tied, he looked at Sara.

'Raise the leg of your breeches,' he told her.

Sara raised it again.

'First, I shall apply the compress. Then I shall give you some medicine to take. This you must take every hour for the next six hours. Do you understand?'

Sara nodded.

A few moments later, Doctor Zhao had cleaned Sara's leg, applied the compress and tied a bandage. The compress felt warm and Sara's leg began pulsating.

'Stand up, please!' Doctor Zhao told her.

Sara stood.

'Good. I anticipate no problems,' he said and turned his eyes away from the bandage. He looked at Sara's face and frowned. 'But your eyes are dim,' he said. 'Quite dim indeed. Is everything alright?'

Sara's bottom lip trembled.

No, she thought, she wasn't going to cry. Nevertheless, her eyes misted as the tears welled up in them…

# CHAPTER 28

—

The doctor's concern was almost too much to bear. Sara felt that any second, her whole story was going to come pouring out: what had happened in the museum, how she came to be in the painting, how alone and far from home she felt. She opened her mouth; then shook her head, sniffed, wiped a hand across her damp eyes, and straightened herself.

'Well?' Doctor Zhao said. 'There is clearly something bothering you. I wouldn't be the Imperial doctor if I couldn't see that.'

'You wouldn't believe me if I told you.'

'I believe many things you wouldn't believe I believe!' he snapped.

'It doesn't matter. Forget it.'

Doctor Zhao pulled at his moustache. 'I cannot forget what I have not been told, can I?'

'I mean, don't worry about it,' Sara said.

'Don't *worry* about it? Why should I *worry* about it?'

Sara could see this wasn't helping. 'I need to get home. That's all. I just need to get home. But I've got to take this,' she pointed to the saddlebag, 'to someone and tell her it came from Zhang Guolao so that she'll help me.' Sara paused. The doctor's face had flickered at the mention of that name.

'And?' the doctor asked, his face returning to normal.

'And I've no idea where to find her…' Sara could feel her lip tremble again.

'Listen to me,' the Imperial doctor said firmly, 'and I will tell you what you must do. Will you listen?'

Sara nodded. She really was ready to hear anything that might help.

'You must burn some incense,' Doctor Zhao said, looking pleased with himself.

Had she misheard? 'Er… did you say burn incense sticks?'

The doctor nodded sagely.

She took a deep breath and held it. *Well, why didn't I think of that? Burn a couple of sticks and that'll solve all your problems, just like that!*

'I can see you do not understand. But I assure you my reasoning is sound. Do you know of Hsün Tzu?'

She shook her head. This was a waste of time.

'Such ignorance!' Doctor Zhao exclaimed, slipping his hands into his sleeves. She opened her mouth, but Doctor Zhao continued. 'Hsün Tzu said, "Through Ritual, Heaven and Earth join in harmony, the sun and the moon shine, the four seasons arrive, the stars and constellations march, and the rivers flow." Ritual, my dear. Ritual. You must show respect for your ancestors and burn incense – for the Tao leads us all home.'

She stared at the doctor. *HOME.* The word floated in her head. More than anything she had ever wanted in her life, she wanted to go home, wanted to be with her mother and father, wanted to be in Granny Tang's apartment, wanted to listen to Granny Tang's tales, wanted to be back where she belonged, be back where she was happy.

She looked away. The truth was, she felt ashamed. She had been bored by Granny Tang's stories – that was why she had lied and not gone there. But the problem, she suddenly saw, hadn't really been the tales that Granny Tang told, or Granny Tang herself, it hadn't been elsewhere. The problem, she now understood, was how she thought about the stories. The problem, in other words, had been with her. Nevertheless, the idea that burning a couple of incense sticks could get her out of the picture and send her home was… well, ludicrous.

'Are you feeling well enough to walk?' asked Doctor Zhao.

She nodded.

'I have another patient soon,' he said. 'I must prepare.'

'Thank you,' Sara said.

'You are welcome,' the doctor replied and led Sara out of the consultation room. Doctor Zhao's face became serious. 'I must prepare,' he said again.

'Yes, of course. I should be going.' She swung the saddlebag onto her shoulder as the doctor opened the front door.

'By the way,' the doctor said, 'who is the person you are supposed to take the saddlebag to?'

'Wan Yi. I only know that she's a silk merchant and—'

'Well, if you hurry, you might catch her.'

'What?'

For the first time since she had met him, the doctor gave a little smile. 'The person who paid for your treatment? The one who was here before you? That was Wan Yi.'

# Chapter 29

How different everything was! When she had gone into the Imperial doctor's the sun had been high, the shadows short, and the street full of people. But now the street was quieter, the shadows were deep and there were even one or two lanterns burning in windows. She shivered. The air felt chilled. Where had the time gone?

As soon as the doctor had told her that Wan Yi was the woman in the beautiful dress, Sara had run into the street, but there was no sign of Wan Yi. Still, the doctor had an address, which he had reluctantly given to Sara. Now she knew where Wan Yi lived and her leg felt better. Thank goodness! All she had to do was go to the address and give the piece of silk to Wan Yi and Wan Yi would tell her how to get home. Simple! Easy! No problem! After all, why wouldn't an ancient Chinese silk merchant know about time travel? Why wouldn't she be able to solve a puzzle that would baffle Einstein? She was the smartest person in Bianjing!

Although Wan Yi was the best hope Sara had, and although she tried to cling to it, she couldn't. The idea of being stuck in the painting forever and never seeing her family or friends again overwhelmed her. She swallowed hard. Not for the first time, she wondered why all of this had happened to her. A tear trickled down her cheek. She wiped it away angrily.

'Stop it!' she told herself. 'I've been lucky. The boat saved me from Mo Zei's gang, the storyteller gave me food, and the doctor agreed to treat me. I was an arm's length away from Wan Yi and now

I have her address. Be positive! Things could be worse. They often are in nightmares.' She gulped. She really hoped it wasn't going to turn into one of her nightmares. *No! That won't happen!* She would get out of the painting sooner or—

Suddenly something grabbed her neck and pulled her sideways so hard and so fast that both of her legs were lifted off the ground. Kicking like mad, Sara tried to escape, but she was heaved through the air until – *THUMP!* She was dumped on the ground like a bag of rubbish. Her neck was locked in someone's arm. She twisted her head around. She gazed in astonishment at what she saw.

The terrifying face of Mo Zei was grinning back at her.

Mo Zei tightened his arm around Sara's neck. 'Give it to me!' he breathed in her ear. 'Give me the silk.'

Sara struggled in vain. 'You're choking me,' she managed to gasp. Already, blackness was fogging her mind, shutting down her brain…

'We followed the old man for three weeks,' Mo Zei was saying. 'He slipped through our grasp at a great market in Urumqi. Now our journey ends here. Now the silk is finally ours.'

Sara knew she was about to faint. She also knew that if she did, Mo Zei would take the piece of silk and her mission to return it to Wan Yi would have failed. Sara yanked as hard as she could on Mo Zei's little finger.

'Arrrgghhh!' he yelled, loosening his grip around Sara's neck just a little. It was enough for Sara to sink her teeth deep into his arm.

'Arrrrgghh!' Mo Zei yelled again.

Sara reached forward, grabbed a handful of sand, and launched it into his face. 'Arrrrgghh!' he cried for a third time. Blinded by the pain, Mo Zei released Sara.

She rolled away and looked up – the big man from the market was lumbering along the road towards them, two hands stretched in front of him like Frankenstein's monster. She kept on rolling and jumped to her feet. The man lunged towards her. But Sara ducked and his fat hands caught nothing but air.

'GET HER!' roared Mo Zei, on his knees and still wiping sand from his eyes.

Sara's legs moved like pistons. If her leg was still sore, she wasn't feeling it. She flew along the street, looking left and right for someone to help her. Where was everyone? In the dusky stillness, closed doors and the yellow lights from lanterns in windows met her wild stares. She needed to get onto another street – a busier one.

She looked behind. She wished she hadn't. Two dark figures were charging towards her through the gloom. The taller one, Mo Zei, had drawn his sword and was waving it furiously above his head. Sara raced forward, running like she had never run before. A corner up ahead. She skidded around it. Then another. She turned into a street with other people on it. Yes! In front of her, lit by the flickering flames of a fire, a group of men were standing at a stall. They hadn't noticed her. She could shout, scream for help, but between the men and Sara was a sedan chair. She glanced behind her. Mo Zei and his friend hadn't turned the corner yet. This was her chance. She dived into the sedan chair, closed the door, and pulled the curtain. With any luck, Mo Zei and his friend would continue along the street and not look inside.

'What do you think you are doing?'

Panting madly, Sara stared at the woman sitting opposite her.

'I said, what are you doing?'

'You!' cried Sara, staring into the almond eyes of Wan Yi.

'I asked you what you are doing.'

'I'm not a robber,' wheezed Sara.

'I'm glad to hear it,' Wan Yi replied. 'For your sake.' She shifted, and Sara noticed the small dagger in her hand, the silver blade only partially covered by her silk robe.

'I met you in the doctor's house. I need to give you something! There are two men chasing me. They're after it too, but it's yours.'

Just then, they heard men's voices.

'Where is she, boss?' It could only be Mo Zei's friend.

Sara shrunk back. She had never felt more frightened in her life. Her heart seemed to have grown to the size of a hot air balloon.

'She may have doubled back.' Mo Zei this time.

'What shall I do, boss?'

'Go back. See if you can find her. I'll continue.'

Sara listened, holding her breath. Footsteps went past the sedan. Other footsteps, heavier ones, padded past and retreated. Slowly, the sounds grew distant and finally disappeared.

When they were gone, Wan Yi gave Sara a hard look. 'What is all this about?'

'I promised I would bring this to you,' Sara said, holding up the saddlebag.

'Who gave you this?' Wan Yi asked.

'Zhang Guolao. I was on the road and his horse threw him off. Mo Zei's gang were coming and Zhang Guolao gave me the saddlebag and told me to give it to you.'

'And you agreed?'

'I had no choice.'

'And where is Zhang Guolao?'

'I think they killed him – Mo Zei and his gang. They came on their horses. I had to escape.'

'Zhang Guolao is dead?' Wan Yi whispered.

Sara rested the saddlebag on her lap. 'I'm sorry,' she said.

Wan Yi's eyes narrowed and a look of cold fury hardened her face. 'Mo Zei will pay,' she said through clenched teeth. 'I will make sure of it.'

Sara did not doubt it.

'How did you escape?' Wan Yi asked.

'I jumped into the river.'

'The river?'

'A man in a rowing boat pulled me in. He took me to a ship, but it wasn't going to Bianjing. So I escaped from that as well because Zhang Guolao told me that you were in Bianjing.'

'I see. So why did you bring the saddlebag? Why not just steal its contents?'

'I'm not a thief! And anyway, I promised Zhang Guolao I'd do it. But he also told me you were the smartest person in the city and I need help… Though to be honest, I don't think anyone can solve my problem.'

Wan Yi tilted her head. 'We shall see. So why did you not come to me immediately?'

'Because Zhang Guolao didn't tell me exactly where I could find you. I've been looking for you since I arrived in Bianjing.'

'Poor you!' Wan Yi said, squeezing Sara's hand. 'Well, you've found me at last, and now it is time to see what Zhang Guolao entrusted you with.'

# CHAPTER 30

—

'May I?' said Wan Yi, reaching out a delicate hand towards the unopened saddlebag.

Sara handed the precious bag to Wan Yi, glad to be done with the responsibility of keeping it safe.

Eyes shining, Wan Yi reached in and brought out the piece of silk. 'It's even more beautiful than I imagined,' she breathed, pulling back the curtain and turning it towards the light that shone from the brazier. 'Magnificent.'

'Are you going to use it to make something? A lady's handkerchief?'

Wan Yi gave a hoot of laughter, but immediately glanced at Sara and covered her mouth with her hand. 'I beg your pardon,' she said. 'I should not have laughed. That was very rude.'

Sara shrugged. 'Is it too valuable to make into something?'

'It is very valuable, yes. In fact, there is nothing else quite like it. And there is no need to make it into something else. It already is what it is.'

*More riddles,* thought Sara.

'Now watch,' Wan Yi said. She was holding the piece of silk at one corner, pinching it between her thumb and forefinger. She flicked her wrist, once, twice, three times. The silk darted in the air, back and forth. Once, twice…

Sara gasped.

The dragons and puzzle balls decorating the piece of silk were still there, but the ordinary, square-shaped piece of fabric had gone.

In its place was a dagger – a hilt, around which Wan Yi's slender fingers were wrapped, with a lethal-looking, double-edged blade. Its pattern and colours glistened like liquid metal.

Wan Yi was holding a silk dagger!

'That's not… That's impossible,' Sara breathed, reaching out a hand.

'Careful,' Wan Yi said quickly. 'Do not touch the blade. The slightest pressure on its edge is enough to cut to the bone.'

Sara gingerly touched the hilt instead. It was solid. Unyielding. Real. 'But how…?'

Wan Yi flicked her wrist again. As if it had never been anything else, the piece of silk crumpled. 'It's yours,' she said.

'Er… Well…'

Wan Yi took Sara's hand and dropped the piece of silk into it before Sara could pull it away. 'Take it,' she said.

'Wow! Wait a minute! Why are you giving it to me? Zhang Guolao wanted you to have it.' She pushed her hand towards Wan Yi, but Wan Yi shoved it back again.

'It will not become a dagger until you are three,' she said.

Sara raised her eyebrows. 'Three? I'm 14 years old!'

Wan Yi smiled and closed Sara's hand around the piece of silk. 'It will not become a dagger until you are three.' Sara opened her mouth to ask what she meant, but before she could, Wan Yi held up a hand. 'All will become clear. Now, put it away in your pocket.'

Sara did as she was told.

Wan Yi grinned. 'It's time to see if the smartest woman in Bianjing can help you.'

# CHAPTER 31

—

After Wan Yi gave her the silk dagger, she had listened patiently to Sara's tale. Sara felt a little foolish telling it. At the same time, she was pleased that Wan Yi followed her every word. At the end, Wan Yi was silent for what seemed a long time, gazing out of the sedan at the quiet streets. Finally, she had faced Sara and said she agreed with the doctor. Sara needed to burn some incense.

*Burn some incense sticks! What good would that do?* Sara wondered. But she hadn't said anything. She'd burn the sticks – whatever! There was no Plan B, so she might as well.

Wan Yi's sedan took Sara to the incense stall where she bought the sticks with the money the storyteller had given her. Then they went to the nearest temple graveyard. It didn't take long, but early evening was fast approaching and stars were appearing overhead.

Now, as Sara looked out of the sedan into the gloaming, a monk dressed in long robes was walking slowly towards the front gate of the temple, a lantern in his hand.

'That is Lao An,' said Wan Yi. 'He will help us now.'

Lao An greeted them with a bow. Wan Yi stood a little behind Sara, watching. 'Have you come for the Qingming festival?' he asked, addressing Sara.

'Yes,' she answered, remembering that the Qingming festival, which was shown in the scroll, was about respecting one's elders and honouring one's ancestors.

'Then please come in,' the monk said, and she entered the gate to the graveyard and walked on the cobble-stone path beside the monk while Wan Yi walked behind.

Inside, the graveyard was busy with people paying their respects. Some were making offerings of food, tea, wine, or chopsticks. Others burned paper money. The air was thick with the pungent smoke that rose from burning joss sticks. The rich smell of the incense reminded Sara of her visits to the temples in Beijing. Entire families would come to them, even young children, and work together to sweep away the leaves, weed the plots, and add fresh soil to the graves.

There were many kinds of graves. Some looked like brick square-based pagodas of different heights. Others were slabs of black stone, covered with inscriptions. Some had *shishi* lions on either side like bookends while others were simple stones the size of shoe boxes, with only the Chinese characters of the person's name.

Sara noticed a grave that was covered with leaves and weeds. It seemed that no one had visited it in a long while. The monk followed her eyes.

'The Qingming festival is a time to keep alive our memories of our ancestors through the observance of rites. It saddens me to think of the poor soul lying there forgotten.'

Sara thought of her grandfather's grave, of the small plot where generations of her own family lay. She also thought about her grandmother, who often requested that Sara come and spend some time with her taking care of the grave. In the past, Sara had always found an excuse not to. But that would change. If she ever got out of this mess, she would help Granny Tang.

Sara looked at the characters written on the headstone. They looked similar to the Mandarin she'd learned at school, but were different enough that she wasn't sure what they meant. 'I'm sorry. I can't read this,' she said. 'What was this person's name?'

The monk read the stone to her. 'Lao Tuzi,' he said. 'His grave has been here since I first came many years ago. I do not know his family.' He shook his head slowly. 'It is said that to forget one's ancestors is to be a brook without a source, a tree without a root. Such a shame.'

'May I?' Sara asked, reaching out for the broom.

The monk handed it to her, bowed, and walked away quietly, leaving Sara and Wan Yi alone.

'I want to sweep the grave,' Sara said.

Wan Yi nodded. 'I shall hold up the lantern.'

Broom in hand, Sara went to work, first sweeping, tidying and cleaning. When at last she was finished, she looked at Wan Yi, who smiled. All the other people seemed to have left and it was just Wan Yi, the monk and herself in the graveyard silence. Sara propped the broom up against a tree and stretched. Her hands were sore and her back ached, but she felt at peace. For a moment, she stared at the heavens above, the distant stars that shimmered, brilliant multitudes in the darkness. The photons from some had taken thousands, millions, even billions of years to reach Earth. If you thought about it, the whole night sky was a giant time machine, and time travel was possible just by looking up at the stars...

Behind her, there was a cough from Wan Yi, and Sara's mind floated back to the graveyard. The incense sticks in her pocket! Kneeling down, she placed them in a pot, and with a burning taper from the monk, lit them. Their tips burned red for a second before she blew on them, extinguishing the flames so that they smouldered and gently loosened their fragrant smoke. She stood and bowed to the grave. 'Rest well, Lao Tuzi,' she said.

Something rustled nearby. Suddenly, a hare bounced out of one of the shrubs ringing the graveyard. Sara almost screamed in surprise. The hare hopped a few metres, stopped and stood up on its hind legs next to the headstone, peering straight at her. Sara admired its long, elegant ears, and its dark, shining eyes. *There are rabbits and hares everywhere,* she thought – *here, in the story-teller's tale about Confucius, even on the door of Madam Zhong's wooden shack!*

The hare was sitting motionless; only its twitching whiskers moved. The temple had grown so quiet Sara could hear the crickets chirping from across the rice paddies. All of a sudden, the hare stood on its hind legs and tilted its head to one side as if in thought. Sara knelt down slowly before it. The hare stayed upright, eyeing her as she drew closer. Sara put her hand out and stroked its ears. The hare leaned into her, allowing her to pet its head.

'It's so beautiful,' Sara said. 'I can't believe it's not running away.'

Wan Yi said, 'Animals give us different eyes to see with. This hare seems to see something in you, maybe something you cannot even see yourself.'

Sara looked deeply into the hare's eyes. *What makes it look so smart?* she wondered. *If it could speak, what would it tell me?*

'It is said there are people who can speak with animals,' Wan Yi said. 'They have learned nature's languages. They listen to mountains, talk to fire. They tell us the stories of the stars and the moon.'

The hare in front of Sara turned to face Wan Yi.

'Just look,' Wan Yi said, pointing to the moon, as pale and round as a peeled lychee. 'The Jade Rabbit is the companion of the Moon Goddess Chang'e, and uses a mortar and pestle to pound out the elixir of life for the Immortals.'

'Immortals?' Sara asked. She remembered Granny Tang had told her something like that in one of her stories.

'The Eight Immortals. You are familiar with them, yes?' she asked.

'Well, yes,' she answered, wishing she could say so with more conviction. 'I mean, I've heard about them.'

'In ancient times, there was no intermingling between Heaven and Earth. But then there appeared the first shamans. These masters devoted themselves selflessly to their learning. They had virtue and humility. But after them, others came. They sought to place themselves alongside the Immortals.'

Sara thought she remembered a story that went something like this. 'How?' she asked.

'The first shamans were skilled at invoking the gods, at performing the rites and sacrifices that pleased them. It was a source of power, great power. Great shamans like Tian Lan used it wisely. Others did not.' Wan Yi's voice was hushed, but Sara could feel the urgency in her words. 'The hunt for revenge corrupts the seeker; it twists the soul and darkens the heart. Such was the fate of Shan Wu.'

At the sound of the name Shan Wu, the hare, which had been nuzzling at Sara's hand, leaped away.

*Shan Wu,* thought Sara – the name she had heard when she had been transported to that cave where the floating boy had appeared. The thought of the boy's face, his cold tongue, made her shiver. She turned. 'I know that name, Wan Yi,' she said. 'I've seen him.'

'Sara?' A voice behind her, but it did not belong to Wan Yi.

Sara turned again.

What she saw made her gasp.

# CHAPTER 32

'How?' Sara cried, staring at Zhang Guolao's wrinkled face and dusty clothes and his neck. His neck! Where was the wound she had seen Mo Zei inflict? 'That's impossible! I saw them...'

'I am not dead because I cannot be killed.'

Sara shook her head. Another stupid riddle! She looked at Wan Yi, then Zhang Guolao. A hot river of anger was rising and there was nothing she could do about it. This was the last straw – she'd risked her life carrying out what she thought was his dying wish, and they were playing games? Having a laugh? 'Will someone *please* tell me what's going on?' she cried, only just realising that the monk had disappeared.

Wan Yi put an arm around Sara's shoulders. 'We need your help, Sara. What must be done cannot be achieved without you. You are our first hare we have brought to our world. Chan and his... confederates must be defeated.'

*Hare?* thought Sara. *Chan? The Chan in Bai Lu?* she almost asked but didn't. Instead, she shrugged off Wan Yi's arm. 'All of this,' she motioned with her hands to the graveyard, the moon, the night, 'is *your* doing? *You* brought me here?' Her eyes flitted between Zhang Guolao and Wan Yi.

'We had to,' Zhang Guolao said.

'You *had* to? Why?' Sara didn't know which feeling was stronger – her curiosity or her anger. 'Actually, just get me home! I want to go. Now!'

'Has it been that bad?' Wan Yi asked. There was an edge to her voice.

'Why would you even ask that? You think it's been *fun* for me?'

'That's not what I said. I just wondered if it had been *that* bad. After all, you have benefited too.'

She stared at Wan Yi, who stared steadily back at her. Sara shrugged. 'Alright. Can you just tell me what this is all about. I'm sure it's going to be *fascinating*.'

It was Zhang Guolao who spoke. 'You're angry, and you may have a right—'

Sara opened her mouth to speak but had no idea what to say.

'You did very well in the trial we placed you in,' Zhang Guolao continued. 'You showed us your ability to make and execute plans, to be resilient to pain and discomfort, to develop your loyalty and honesty.'

'Like I need training. Do I look like a Labrador?' Sara couldn't help herself.

'Well,' Wan Yi said, 'you've not exactly excelled lately, have you?'

'What's that supposed to mean?'

'Your grandmother in Beijing.'

Before Sara could reply, Zhang Guolao said, 'Look what you did here in this place. You made a great plan. You overcame problems. You acted with integrity. You have the qualities we desire.'

'Just who *are* you?' Sara asked.

'My name is He Xiangu,' Wan Yi said, 'and his name is Zhang Guolao. You may have heard of us.'

Sara was just about to say something rude like, 'Why should I have heard of you? It's not like you're famous'. But then the penny dropped. And when it dropped, her chin followed. 'Zhang Guolao. The Eight Immortals,' Sara whispered.

He Xiangu and Zhang Guolao smiled.

'The Eight Immortals,' Sara repeated. 'But there are only two of you.' She cringed. What a thing to say! Here she was standing in front of two celestial beings, denizens of the Jade Palace, the place where the Eight Immortals reside. And what does she do? She quibbles about numbers! Sara was relieved when He Xiangu laughed.

'You will meet the others soon,' she said. 'For the moment, it is just us. It is a pleasure to meet you properly, Sara Livingstone,' she said and put an arm around Sara's shoulder. This time, Sara didn't shrug it off.

'You must take great care of the silk dagger I gave you,' He Xiangu continued.

At the mention of the piece of silk she had stuffed into the pocket of her breeches, Sara almost flinched. 'You still haven't told me why I need it.' She eyed her pocket warily, half-expecting the dagger's blade to pierce her thigh.

He Xiangu merely smiled sadly.

'We have something else for you too,' Zhang Guolao said, and reaching out, he took hold of Sara's hand.

'Not another dagger!' was Sara's immediate reaction. It wasn't. By the light of the yellow lantern, Sara stared at the object Zhang Guolao had placed in her hand. Heavy and silvery, it was shaped like a slice from a large coin: one edge was smooth and rounded, the other two, which met to form a pointed end, were ragged. There was something embossed on one side. Tilting the silvery shard to the light, Sara could see it was a hare, one of its long ears stretched to the shard's pointed end; its legs ran along the shard's curved edge. It was beautiful…

Still holding the silvery shard, Sara asked, 'Why am I even here? You're Immortals; you can do anything. Why do you need *me*? I'm just an ordinary person. It's not like I have any special powers.'

He Xiangu gave an enigmatic smile. 'You can call us spirits.'

Sara waited. He Xiangu said nothing more.

'Okay… so what's that supposed to mean?'

'I'm sorry but now it is time to go home,' He Xiangu said.

'I want to go home, but you have to tell me what all this is about. You can't just—'

'Remember: you are the first hare. Find the other two,' He Xiangu said. 'Together, you are strong.'

'What do you mean—?' But before she could finish her sentence, Sara felt her feet start to lift off the ground. 'No! Wait!' she cried, stuffing the silvery shard into the pocket of her breeches. 'Not now! Put me down! You have to tell me what's going on! I've got a right to know. Please put me down!' Desperately, she reached down, trying to dig her nails into the damp earth. But it was useless; she was lighter than a feather, lighter than air, and the damp earth slipped through her fingers as she continued floating upwards. A second later, leaves and twigs slipped past her face. She reached out and tried to grab at the branches. They too slipped through her hands. Like a puff of smoke, she was rising higher and higher! She looked down. Everything was so small… She was about to yell again, but then she began to rotate. She turned a somersault, then another and another. 'Arrrgghh!' she screamed. But round and round she went, turning faster and faster, spinning like a wheel…

# Chapter 33

—

'Great. She's alive. *Now* can we get some lunch?'

Sara knew that voice.

'Shut up, Tony!'

Sara knew that one too: Lily's!

'Stand back, everyone. Give her some space. Give her some air.' Ms Ling's.

The first thing Sara saw when she opened her eyes was a ring of faces peering down at her.

'Are you okay?' Ms Ling asked, placing her hand on Sara's brow.

Sara blinked. 'What happened?'

'Dropped like a stone!' sniggered Francis.

'Be quiet!' snapped Ms Ling.

'You fainted,' said Lily, holding Sara's hand. 'But I caught you... Well, almost.'

'Did you have breakfast this morning before you came to school?' asked Ms Ling.

'Oh! She's better. That's good,' the guide said.

'Sara?' It was Ms Ling again. 'Did you have breakfast?'

Sara looked up at Ms Ling. 'I think so, yes.' She wasn't sure. It seemed like such a long time ago and her head felt a bit fuzzy. Things were swirling around it like birds in a storm...

Sara grimaced. She was lying on the cold museum floor and feeling like a fool. Fortunately, the other visitors, who had been amongst the faces peering down at her, were moving away, returning to their own conversations, as were The Gerbil, Jaz, and the Ferdinand brothers. She tried to gather her thoughts.

'I've already called your mum. She's going straight to the hospital.' Ms Ling again.

'How long was I unconscious?' she asked.

'Less than ten minutes,' Ms Ling answered. 'Are you feeling sick?'

'No.' She lifted her head off the floor a fraction. Reaching round, she touched the egg-shaped lump there and winced.

'I didn't do a very good job of catching you. Sorry! I'm so sorry!' Lily cried.

'You hit your head when you fell,' Ms Ling said.

'I feel fine,' Sara protested.

'We were very afraid,' Joaquin said, gazing earnestly at her.

'I'm okay,' Sara said, more gently. 'Honestly.'

'We need to check, just to make sure,' Ms Ling said as the wail of an ambulance grew closer.

Sara, certain she really was fine, sat up, helped by Ms Ling, Lily and Joaquin. A throbbing pain rocked her. 'Ow!' she moaned. 'Shouldn't have done that,' she chuckled.

'Take it *easy*, Sara,' Joaquin said.

'The ambulance has arrived at the outer gate,' the guide said, relaying a message given to him by another man mumbling into a walkie-talkie. 'Two minutes, they'll be here.'

Sara sighed. There was no way Ms Ling, Lily or Joaquin were going to allow her to move before the medical team examined her. She would just wait and be patient and think things through.

What had Francis said? 'Dropped like a stone.' The question was, dropped into *what*? The weirdest dream she had ever had in her life? A hallucination? An alternate universe? Who knew! But at least it was finished. Over and done with. She'd never have to chase some silk merchant across an ancient Chinese city again! Her hallucination, nightmare, fantasy – call it what you liked – was over.

*YES!*

She would have cheered except her head still felt fuzzy and the Ferdinand brothers had had more than enough fun at her expense already.

As soon as Sara saw her mum enter the room at the Chaoyang District Hospital, she cast off the blanket that was draped over her shoulders and strode towards her.

'Poor you!' her mum said, hugging Sara tightly. 'Poor, poor you.'

Sara closed her eyes. Her mum's familiar sweater pressed against her face. 'What happened?' her mum was asking, but Sara didn't want to explain; she didn't want to let go – she didn't ever want to let go.

The nurse who had been waiting with Sara for her mum to arrive spoke instead. 'Well, Sara lost consciousness for a little while and hit her head – but she isn't feeling dizzy or sick, which is good. The hospital has run all the necessary tests just to be sure, but she seems fine.'

'Sara,' her mum said, 'we can go home now.' She waited but Sara hadn't let go. 'Come on, dear,' her mother said, stroking her head. 'Time to go home.'

Finally, Sara loosened her grip. Following her mother's lead, she thanked all the nurses, and with the hospital fees paid, they left the building.

'Car's just over there,' her mother said, pointing to the next row in the car park. 'Can you manage?'

Sara nodded. As she walked beside her mother, she began to feel… uneasy. It was her leg. The top of her thigh. Something was wrong. She glanced down. Her heart missed a beat. Oh no! There was something in her pocket that was rubbing against her leg, something sharp. She shot a look at her mother, who was busy searching for the car keys. Sara gulped. This couldn't be happening! As stealthily as she could, she slipped a hand into her pocket, hoping, hoping, hoping… Her fingertips traced the hard, ragged contours of an object concealed there.

*No!*

She pulled out her hand. No sooner had she done so than she saw her other pocket was bulging slightly. While the car bleeped and unlocked itself, she slipped her hand into the other pocket. Cool, crumpled, soft. 'I don't believe this,' she hissed.

'You alright, dear?' her mother asked, key in hand, gazing at her with a puzzled frown.

'I'm fine! Absolutely fine!'

Her mother shrugged and got in the car. Sara climbed in too. What was going on? She had the coin slice in one pocket and the silk dagger in the other! How was that possible? Hadn't it all just been a horrible, horrible dream? Some sort of super-real, frenzied nightmare? She listened with half an ear for the next forty minutes while her mother talked about the holidays, Granny Tang, the importance of breakfast, how nice Lily and Joaquin were. All the while, the rest of Sara's brain focused on the two objects in her pockets.

She was dying to get back home and take a closer look at them.

After her mum had parked the car and they had taken the lift to their apartment on the 21st floor, Sara followed her mum into the hall of their apartment and stopped outside her bedroom door. From the sitting room, they could hear one of Mrs Ching's soap operas. It was blaring because she liked to listen to them while she hoovered and dusted.

'I'll be back in a moment, honey,' her mum said and went to speak with Mrs Ching. As soon as her mother's back was turned, Sara threw open her bedroom door, and rushing to her computer desk and pulling out the drawer, she stuffed the silvery slice and the piece of silk in and slammed it shut. Just in time. There was knock at the door and her mother came in.

'Just me,' her mother said. The faint sounds of soap opera arguments from the living room could still be heard. Sara sat down on the edge of her bed. Her mother sat next to her.

'So… is there anything you want to tell me?' her mother asked.

Sara couldn't look her mother in the eye. Should she tell her everything? Would she be believed? Would she be taken to a psychiatrist for a mental evaluation? Sara shook her head.

'Are you absolutely sure?' her mother asked.

'I think I was just over-tired, that's all. I didn't get much sleep last night.'

'Well, the hospital seems to think everything is fine… But perhaps we should reschedule our flights to Scotland and go later in the summer?'

'No! Don't do that. I was just tired.' Her mobile phone buzzed with a text from Lily.

'Okay,' her mother said, standing up. 'If you're sure.'

Sara smiled. 'I'm sure.'

'Shall I tell Granny Tang you won't be down to see her before you go?' her mum asked, standing at the door.

'I'm sorry,' Sara said. And she was. She had promised herself she would visit her grandmother more often. But there were other things on her mind right now. Not only that, her time in the scroll had left her feeling completely drained. 'Can I go and see her after the holidays?'

Sara's mum nodded. 'Sure. See you in the morning.'

As soon as her mother had closed the door, Sara gratefully lowered herself, face first, onto her bed. She quickly replied to Lily's text, telling her that the hospital had given her the all clear. Lily was pinging texts at her every two seconds, but Sara told Lily she had to go. Lily made Sara promise to call her in the evening before she boarded her flight, which Sara did.

Putting down the phone, Sara stood and slowly pulled up the leg of her trousers to reveal… Where was the jagged cut running from her knee to her ankle? 'What…?' she whispered, running her fingers up and down and up and down her shin. No pain. No scar. No sign at all that her leg had been badly cut. Either the Imperial doctor was a genius or… Rolling down her trouser leg, she yanked open her desk drawer. Was she mad? Had she imagined finding the objects? Had she imagined putting them in her drawer? But there, lying on an essay she had stuffed into her drawer, was the piece of silk and the silvery slice.

It didn't make sense. How could she *not* have the wound? She picked up the silvery slice and let go of it. It clattered noisily onto the wooden floorboards, just as any piece of metal would. Reaching down, she picked it up and tried to bend it. She couldn't. In her other hand, she picked up the piece of silk and dangled it in front of her eyes, let it tickle her nose, tried to look through it. They were both real. Both had exactly the kind of physical properties that any other piece of metal and any other piece of silk had. So why was there no wound?

She dropped the piece of silk and the silvery slice onto her bed, watching as the silk gently crumpled and the slice bounced a little and settled. She had absolutely *no idea* what the Immortals wanted her to do with these objects. 'Out of a billion people living in China, I've been selected by ancient immortals to… to do what?' she asked herself. 'If the silk and the slice are real, then whatever the Immortals want me to do with them must be pretty important. Fine. But why do they need *me*? Why am *I* so important?'

He Xiangu's words played in her head again: 'You are our first hare. Find the other two.' The other two? So not only did the

Immortals need her help, they needed the help of two more people as well! She collapsed onto the bed, her mind still racing.

The Immortals had mentioned Chan. Was it the same Chan who owned Bai Lu or not? Most probably it was – after all, why else was she having those… er… visions every time she saw his face? So was her mission to fight one of the richest men in the world? She scoffed. If Chan and his confederates – whoever they were – were the enemy, what was she supposed to do? She'd never been in a fight in her life! Who did the Immortals think she was, Wonder Woman?

Reaching over, she held the silvery slice in the palm of her hand. The two Immortals had called her a hare. And there, embossed on one side of this silvery piece of metal, was a hare. What was its significance? Why a hare? Why not a lion? Or a dragon? At least they were heroic!

Her computer was buzzing madly again – a sort of shrieking, high-pitched whine. She glanced at it, puzzled. Then she shrugged, put the slice on the bed, and picked up the piece of silk.

An innocent piece of fabric…

She chewed her lip. The urge was irresistible. She shouldn't. She knew she shouldn't. Nevertheless, she stood up, and leaning over a little, with her feet out of the way in case she dropped it, she closed her eyes and flicked her wrist – once, twice, three times… She opened her eyes.

Nothing. Nothing had happened.

'Okay.' She tried again, this time flicking the silk harder. Again, nothing. She tried holding it by a different corner. Nothing. She tried holding the silk in her left hand. Nothing. Every time she tried it, the same thing happened: nothing. Then she remembered what He Xiangu had said: 'It will not become a dagger until you are three.'

Holding the piece of silk by a corner, she opened her carry-on bag and dropped it between her headphones and the book she was taking for the flight. She did the same with the silvery slice. It suddenly occurred to her that airport security would X-ray her bag. What would she say if they stopped her? She stared at the two objects. She couldn't really explain it, but the thought of being parted from them was not one she liked, even though she hated the fact that the piece of silk was a deadly weapon – at least in He Xiangu's hands! It was as if both were too important to leave behind, too precious not to be an arm's length away… Her skin tingled as a little shiver ran down her spine. Would airport security ask about the slice? Maybe; maybe not. She would cross that bridge when she came to it.

Zipping the bag and shoving it below her bed, she returned to her computer. Thankfully, the buzzy noise had lessened a little. Even so, it was still annoying. She checked the plug. It wasn't hot and neither was the computer. It didn't seem to be an electrical problem. She'd tell her dad in the morning, if she remembered. She yawned again. She would have loved to do some research on Bai Lu and Chan's empire. She would have loved to find out more about the silvery slice. But it wasn't going to happen. Not tonight. Not after everything she'd been through.

Fifteen minutes later, she was in bed, sunk in a deep, dreamless sleep.

# PART 5

# KHOTAN AND THE
# JADE PALACE, CHINA
## NORTHERN SONG DYNASTY
### 996 CE

# CHAPTER 34

---

When he awoke, the sun was overhead. Shan Wu had no idea how far he'd walked. Last night, his anger and his fever had driven him on; his mind had been a tireless horse carrying his body like a wounded rider. The anger he felt was not only at Tian Lan's determination to steer him away from thoughts of revenge. It was also anger at the Immortals, for their indifference to the humans they pushed around. Why would people place their lives in the hands of gods who did not care whether or not their souls were crushed? How could people so blindly accept their fate? These ideas had crowded his mind, leaving no room for anything else.

The light was so bright he could not fully open his eyes. He looked around, expecting to see the small bushes and grasses he had been walking through, but they were nowhere to be found. Instead, there was only sand. Sand in every direction. He turned in the direction from which he thought he'd come. There was no sign of a village. The heat made him incredibly dizzy and he had to cover his eyes with his hands.

Shan Wu suddenly felt the world grow to twice its size – ten times, a hundred times larger, a hundred thousand times larger. He was a grain of sand in a desert without end. Fear entered his heart. Where could he turn? Would the gods save him – if he asked them to? 'Am I truly alone?' he cried to the heavens and waited. The only sound was the wind racing along the sand. That was his answer.

But then when he thought about it, when he truly thought about it, he realised how fortunate he was. It was a sound that would have gone unheard if he had not been standing right there, at that very time. Yes, he was alone. The wind sang its song for him and only him. And the words of the song said there was nothing and no one else he could rely on. For that reason, he would take faith in himself.

Tian Lan was not surprised to find the space next to him empty when he woke that morning. *There is a limit to what one may learn from others,* he thought. *While I am saddened by his suffering, it is a path that he must walk alone. He is in the gods' hands now.* Straightening his robes, he crossed his legs and sat in silent prayer.

Shan Wu could no longer tell the difference between light and heat. The ground he walked on, the air he breathed, the sky above, they all seemed filled with a brightness that cut through him. He had only been walking for two days, yet any area of skin that was not covered by his robe was now red and blistered, too painful to touch. In his water gourd, there were only a few mouthfuls of water remaining. But still he walked, following his feet, one after the other, on and on.

As he walked, doubts circled and re-circled in his mind like vultures. *Every step I have taken has led me here. What if I have taken a false step, if I have gone the wrong way and entered a place from which I cannot return? What if Tian Lan was right? What if I was wrong to leave him?*

Nevertheless, he could not turn back. He had to continue.

The nights were almost as bad as the days. When the sun fell in the west, the temperature would plummet. He would try to sleep, but the cold would creep into his robe, snatch sleep away from him. It made his thoughts more jumbled, more self-pitying, more furious.

At sunrise on the third day of his journey without Tian Lan, after another night of intense cold, he was awakened by his own shivering. He prised his eyelids open and found himself looking up at a man covered from head to foot in a white robe. The only part of his body visible was the open space around his eyes that allowed him to see. He was standing next to a camel which, from the ground, seemed to tower over him.

Shan Wu tried to speak, but the only sounds that came out of his mouth were as wind across the dunes.

The man leaned down and helped him into a sitting position. It was only after Shan Wu was upright that he noticed the man was not alone. There were others, maybe a dozen riders, a short distance off. Each was dressed the same way, in flowing robes. Long, curved swords hung at their sides. Scarves covered their heads so he could not see their faces, only their eyes. They were all riding camels, sitting on red blankets with many tassels. Brightly coloured tassels decorated the camels' heads as well. Some of the beasts were carrying large bags, but all were loosely linked together with a slack rope so that they formed a ragged train.

The man in front of him pulled the scarf from his face and said something, words that Shan Wu knew but did not understand. The man pushed a skin bag up to Shan Wu's mouth, pressing the opening against his lips. The water was so delicious, Shan Wu felt as if he were tasting it for the first time. The man allowed him to take several gulps before removing the bag. The man began speaking again. This time Shan Wu was able to make out some of what he said.

'Where are you going?' the man asked.

'The next village,' Shan Wu answered.

'The nearest village is four days by camel,' the man said.

'Which direction?'

The man pointed towards the western horizon. 'Impossible to walk. You will die.'

Shan Wu stared out at the horizon. The waves of heat coming off the sand made it ripple like water in a fast-flowing river. One of the men in the group shouted something and pointed up at the sun. He looked at the man near him.

'Come. You will ride one of the camels we will sell,' the man said. He pulled Shan Wu to his feet. 'I am called Ahmed. Your name?'

'Shan Wu.'

Ahmed looked at Shan Wu's sunburned face, his tattered robes. 'Well, let us journey to Khotan together.'

# CHAPTER 35

For Shan Wu, the journey to Khotan was a blur. Lost in large empty spaces inside himself, he was barely aware of the passing of time. The camel he rode rocked in a hypnotic rhythm that sent him down a chasm, to a place where the heat and light of the desert could not reach him. Finally, the caravan stopped for the day in a small, dusty village – though for Shan Wu, it seemed not to have moved at all.

That night, Shan Wu woke up with a start. He looked around the chamber where he lay – a cramped, unadorned room next to the stables. On the floor, wrapped in their gowns, their swords at their sides, the members of the caravan slept, a few of them snoring loudly.

Shan Wu listened. Something had wakened him. What had it been? He tried to fathom the reason. As he lay, hardly breathing, a certainty grew within him: he had been summoned. It was as if a wordless voice that he could not hear had called him. He stood up and crossed the room, taking care not to awaken any of the others. He walked out of the stables and into the courtyard.

Outside, only the stars and a gibbous moon greeted him. In the distance, a temple bell rang. The sound of it echoed across the night and died. But inside Shan Wu's head, the chime grew louder and louder until it seemed it would shatter his skull. It was as if he had opened his mouth underwater and his soul was pouring back into his body. His memories rushed in, filling him with a sense of self – memories of the village, his father and mother, his younger brother, the burial of Gong Liu.

He recalled his mother's warm embrace, the sweet smell of the rice pot, the stickiness of the rice as he scraped the bottom with his fingers. Again he heard his father's voice, as clear as if he were standing there next to him. And there was Shan Tuo, by his side, smiling. He longed to be back with his family, to be huddled around the fire at night, watching their faces as they ate, listening to their happy chattering.

But the scene slowly dissolved in his mind, and in its place came a feeling of emptiness, but not calm. Instead, it was the stillness that comes when the earth holds its breath and waits for the onslaught of a storm. It was a lull in which great, unseen – and as yet unfelt – forces were gathering. And the storm was rising in him. Memories and questions in a blizzard of words and images flew around his head: his father's tattoo, Baojun's retainers, the empty village.

Why had his family been taken away from him? Why? Why? Why? And as the questions multiplied, so the anger in him rose and rose once again, sweeping away everything in its path. Fate had brought him nothing but misery, nothing but death and loss and betrayal. Yes, betrayal. That was what he felt. Betrayed by fate. His heart pounded, his fists tightened.

And yet… he saw Tian Lan's face, his stern expression, kind eyes and generosity. Had not fate brought him too? Had not fate, through Tian Lan, offered him another path?

The next morning at dawn, for the first time since he had left Tian Lan, Shan Wu re-entered the world beyond to seek Tian Lan. He had told himself he would not do so, would not try to contact him. But his body had known his own, deeper desires better. It had woken him moments before the sun's first rays had split the horizon and Shan Wu, acknowledging the need, had immediately entered the other world.

At first, he thought his other world had become even darker, but then he realised he was inside a badly lit room. A smoky candle burned next to the room's only bed where, beneath a thin blanket, someone lay motionless. As Shan Wu watched, an old woman came into the room. Shan Wu recognised her: the woman from the village who had provided them with food and shelter. He remembered how caring she had been, how she had offered freely of what little she had. Of course, this was the world beyond and she took no notice of Shan Wu because she could not see him. She was carrying a tray with a bowl of thin soup on it. A rice ball sat next to it on a small plate. She placed both on a low table next to the shape under the blanket.

'Does our honoured guest feel any better?' she asked.

Shan Wu was not surprised he now understood her words. The world beyond had its own rules: distances and times shortened and lengthened, often in erratic and unexpected ways; objects appeared and disappeared, or sometimes lingered, mere outlines. And as for languages, there were none he could not understand in the world beyond.

As he watched, the shape beneath the blanket stirred as a face emerged. The candle flickered.

'Thank you, but I am not hungry,' Tian Lan said, eyeing the bowl.

'I have brought you some soup,' the old woman said, and a mocking smile played on Shan Wu's face. In the real world, it was clear that Tian Lan had not had time to learn the meaning of the old woman's words: each was talking but neither understood the other.

The old woman tugged on Tian Lan's arms, pulling him up until he rested on his elbows. Shan Wu was amazed at how much Tian Lan had aged since the last time they were together. His eyes seemed sunken, his skin the colour of ash.

'Don't spill it,' she said and spooned some soup into Tian Lan's mouth, which he had reluctantly opened. It seemed to cause him pain to swallow. After a few more spoonfuls, Tian Lan held up a hand.

'I cannot,' he said.

'We pray for your return to health, sir.'

Tian Lan slumped back down on the bed and stared at the ceiling, his breath coming in short gasps. The old woman took another blanket and gently placed it on top of him. Then she cleaned up her things and left the room. As soon as she was gone, Shan Wu, his other self moving like a ghostly shadow, drew closer to Tian Lan. While he had been completely invisible to the old woman, Tian Lan reacted to him immediately.

'Shan Wu,' he said simply, his voice a husk of what it had been. 'Know that I am nearing the end of this path. When I pass through the door, it will be the last time. I will not return.' He grimaced but continued. 'I thank you for seeing my spirit off. It was my wish to see you again.' He coughed for a few moments. And then it was over. The lines in his face grew smooth and his expression became peaceful. Shan Wu watched the old man's spirit depart, a light that radiated from the body for several heartbeats before disappearing.

As Shan Wu sat next to Tian Lan's body, a profound sadness filled him. But like the sadness he had felt when his father and mother had died, it faded, and an all-consuming darkness welled up from inside his heart.

*Tian Lan was a victim*, he thought, *of a desire to do good.*

Shan Wu would be nobody's victim.

The caravan of riders and beasts set out an hour after dawn for the final stage of its journey to Khotan. Before, when he was Shan Mu, he had been a son who had behaved, who had conformed like everyone else, who had *looked* as if he knew his destiny and was happy to be led. But that was then. Now he knew his own way. Now he was himself. Now he was Shan Wu.

# CHAPTER 36

—

The swaying camel lumbered to a stop. Shan Wu looked up to see a great many camels amassed in the narrow road, waiting. Across the tawny, shimmering desert plain, the towers of a large city rose like fingers amidst the palm trees that filled the oasis. It was late afternoon. The day's fierce heat had mellowed, the shadows were slowly lengthening and deepening, and the sun's rays were growing more slanted and yellow.

'I rode beside you, mostly to keep you from falling out of your saddle,' Ahmed said. 'You had much to say in your sleep.' Shan Wu could see something new in Ahmed's eyes. They mirrored a change he noticed in himself. He felt different somehow, in a way he did not yet understand.

They entered the city gate. 'Welcome to Khotan,' Ahmed said. 'You may know it as Hotan. It is a trading centre that the oasis has helped grow big. There are many travellers – some bring things to sell, others stay to open shops. You will find anything you want here.'

A bustling city, Khotan was situated along a trade route that had been travelled for many years. The people of the city welcomed foreigners and made it easy for them to sell their goods. Ahmed and his group made for the section where the inns, known as *caravanserai*, were set up amongst a maze of narrow streets that led to the bazaar.

They came to a large ochre building. Ahmed spoke briefly with a young man who came out to meet them. 'Tell Mizben that

Ahmed has returned, bearing treasures from afar,' he said, smiling so broadly his teeth glowed.

The young man disappeared inside the building. A few moments later, a tall man with a pointed beard came out. Ahmed greeted the owner of the *caravanserai*, who welcomed him with open arms.

'Shan Wu,' Ahmed said, gesturing with a flourish to the tall man, 'meet Mizben, the owner of these sumptuous lodgings.'

The man bowed to Shan Wu before turning to Ahmed. 'You have brought what I want?' Mizben asked.

Ahmed flashed his toothy smile again. 'Of course!'

This answer satisfied Mizben greatly. He turned and ushered them through a portal that led to a wide courtyard. Lining the walls were bays for the animals and chambers for the men. The camels were tethered in their stalls, unburdened of their heavy loads, and given feedbags. The men were shown to their rooms.

'I cannot pay,' Shan Wu said.

'Ahmed has vouched for you,' the owner said. 'He believes you will have no problem paying once you get settled.'

Later, after he had rested in a sparse room – furnished only with a table and a pair of rickety chairs, a brass oil light, and a pallet bed with a frayed blanket – night had fallen, and Shan Wu walked out with Ahmed.

'Let us go to see what opportunities the bazaar offers us,' he said.

To Shan Wu, the words were unremarkable, but the tone seemed strange, as though a secret were being hidden amongst them. Nevertheless, he did not question Ahmed, walking beside him silently while absorbing the city's many sights and sounds – some wondrous, some not. On many street corners, starving people sat begging with their cupped hands held in front of their faces as rich people walked past, ignoring them. Shan Wu ignored them too, but one figure – an old woman dressed in rags sitting below a crooked tree on a three-legged stool – caught his eye.

'Wait!' Shan Wu told Ahmed and strode towards where the woman was seated. 'Once again I will have need of your money,' he called over his shoulder. It was not a question.

'Where are you going?' Ahmed cried. Shan Wu ignored him. When he reached the old woman, she looked up at him disdainfully, as though she were about to do *him* a favour. She did not speak. Instead, she picked up the needle on her lap and plunged it into the small, glowing fire next to her, over which she was boiling a pot of water. At her other foot, black ink swam in a shallow bowl. 'What is it you want me to do?' she asked, eyes on the now glowing needle.

With a stick Shan Wu took from the pile the old woman had gathered to keep the fire burning, he drew in the dirt the characters and the design that he wanted – the three serpent-shaped forms that enclosed the phrase top and bottom. When the old woman finally turned around and looked at it, she sniffed.

'Where do you want it?' she asked.

'Start here,' Shan Wu said, pointing to the inside of his forearm near the crease at the elbow, 'and finish here.' He pointed to the skin that lay between his thumb and index finger.

The old woman's eyebrows rose. 'Very visible!'

'Just do it.'

Even at night the bazaar bustled with excitement, as people bought, sold, traded, stole. There were stalls set up holding all sorts of goods, from foodstuffs to gemstones. Ahmed led Shan Wu to a corner of the market and asked him to sit. Then, in a booming voice, he addressed those nearest him.

'We have here a wise master,' Ahmed said, indicating Shan Wu. 'One who has gained great knowledge from his time wandering the Taklamakan. For a small fee, the Seer of the Taklamakan will tell you your future. Come! Do not be shy!'

Ahmed winked at Shan Wu, who stared at him, aghast. What? Who had given him permission to do this? And how had Ahmed come to know anything about him? It made no sense, unless… Shan Wu looked at Ahmed, who was grinning ear to ear. Yes, unless Ahmed truly knew nothing and was only trying to trick people.

Shan Wu opened his mouth, but before he could say anything, a small, round-faced man approached. He was dressed in a white gown and had a white turban wrapped around his head. He sat down in front of Shan Wu. His eyes darted back and forth as if he were hiding from someone. 'I-I need some advice, your holiness,' he said.

Shan Wu looked at Ahmed, who was silently urging him on. Suddenly, looking at that rotund man in the turban, Shan Wu knew. In his heart, it felt as though a lock had turned, a door had opened. An immense power lay before him ready to be grasped, to be used. All he had to do was take it. Had it always been so? Perhaps it had. Perhaps he had known it all along but had lacked the courage – the conviction – to use it, to make it work for *him*.

But now it coursed through him: a thrumming, vibrant river. His fingers, his arms, his whole body shook with it! He gazed in wonder at the crowd. Their every thought was laid bare, their every secret as clear as the moon and stars above them. What he could not see was not worth seeing. That one there, the one with the lazy eye – how his wife hated him! That one with the oversized cap – how he longed to open a barber's shop. That one with the narrow face – how he regretted murdering his cousin. Each stranger's thoughts were like voices shouting in his head. He marvelled at the voices' clarity and insistence. He had been living his life with his fingers in his ears! Well, not any longer. Shan Mu had truly gone. *Look at me! I am Shan Wu! I am the Seer of the Taklamakan. I have come before you! From the chrysalis to the butterfly, I have emerged!* He gazed at the faces gawping at him. These fools, with their meaningless lives, their petty worries! He would live off them, the way a spider feeds on flies!

The man in the white turban was staring at him; Ahmed was still grinning, but only just. Shan Wu reached forward and, taking hold of the man's podgy hand, pulled him closer.

'Let me read the answer in your eyes,' Shan Wu said.

The man leaned towards him and Shan Wu looked deep into his eyes. A picture was forming, one that grew sharper, as if it were emerging from a mist.

'You sold your brother a pair of goats,' Shan Wu announced, so suddenly the man flinched. 'You collected the money from your brother, three silver coins. But you knew that the goats were ill – you had seen them lying on the ground, close to death.'

The man's eyes had grown rounder and rounder and his mouth had fallen open. Shan Wu continued speaking in a hard, fast voice. 'Before you sold the goats to your brother, you fed them a potion, forced it down the animals' throats.'

The man gulped, stammered, tried to pull his hand away, but Shan Wu held on to it tightly and continued. 'The goats became very energetic, so lively that they fooled your brother into believing they were years younger than their actual age. They stayed that way, until the day after he had taken them away, back to his home, where they both died.'

The man finally wrestled his hand free. 'This is not true!' he cried, turning left and right, addressing the small crowd that had gathered around them. 'It's a lie, I tell you.' He turned and looked pleadingly at Ahmed. Ahmed was too stunned to say anything.

Shan Wu sneered. How he hated this pathetic little worm. 'But that is not the worst part,' he said, raising his voice further. 'The illness that the goats carried infected your brother and his family. Even now, they lie in bed, fighting for their lives.'

There was a gasp from the crowd.

'H-how could you possibly know that?' the man cried, his voice shaking.

'I also know that you will say that you do not have enough to pay me. But that will not stop you from giving me every coin in your pocket.' Shan Wu's voice turned even crueller. 'And do not bother to plead that your own wife is ill. Give me your money and leave. Now!'

The man reached into his robe and pulled out a leather satchel. He did not even count the coins but instead he threw the satchel at Ahmed and was soon lost from sight, deep in the bazaar's innards.

Ahmed stared at Shan Wu, a mixture of astonishment and glee on his face.

'Only if he helps us with our problems!' cried a large, bald man, whose rolls of chins beneath his round face were five-fold thick. 'I don't want him raking through *my* dirty laundry!'

The crowd laughed and Ahmed cried, 'My friends, do not worry. The Seer of the Taklamakan is here to help you. Is that not so, master?'

Shan Wu glared at Ahmed.

'Is that not so, master?' Ahmed said again.

Shan Wu nodded. 'Very well.'

'So, come!' cried Ahmed, smiling broadly. 'Let the seer's wisdom guide you! Only three *wen* – a measly price for an infinitude of insight!'

And so, for a few coins at a time, Shan Wu traded his visions for money, giving those who paid knowledge of where to find lost lockets, the cures for minor illnesses, how to rid one's household of a troublesome spirit.

Before long, he and Ahmed had acquired enough money to pay the *caravanserai* owner a month's rent for the use of his rooms.

On their way back from the marketplace, their pockets loaded with the money they had earned that night, Ahmed's curiosity finally overcame his tact and he asked about the tattoo on Shan Wu's arm – as Shan Wu knew he would.

'But only criminals have such things!' Ahmed cried, his face lit by the burning torches adorning the rich men's houses that rose beside the path they were following. 'Are you a criminal?'

'Not only criminals have these.'

'Then who else?'

'Others – men who take oaths.'

'*Establish the hegemon*,' Ahmed muttered darkly, reciting the words of the tattoo on Shan Wu's arm. 'What's a hegemon, anyway?'

'A leader,' Shan Wu replied.

'No! No! No!' Ahmed laughed and slapped Shan Wu on the back. 'My leader is *wen*! Do you hear? *Wen!*' He dug into his pockets and showed the coins in his hand to Shan Wu. 'These are the only leaders we need! Forget about establishing someone who cares nothing for you!'

Shan Wu smiled. 'You misunderstand,' he said quietly. '*I* am the hegemon.'

# CHAPTER 37

━

Another evening two weeks later, Shan Wu was walking the streets, feeling Khotan's energy crackle within him. He let the sounds of the city wash over him: the cry of hawkers selling their wares – bronze pots, ceramic bowls, woven baskets, silks; the squalling babies, the soothing voices of their mothers; the shouts of children chasing one another. Men pulled carts laden with goods; dogs, scavenging for food, ran underfoot; rats peeped out from cracks in the walls. Everywhere was motion.

Shan Wu walked on, weaving through the streets as if mysteriously pulled by a string. He stopped when he reached a wide plaza. His eyes were drawn to the huddled figure of a beggar on the opposite side. The boy was sitting in the dirt in front of a building fallen into disrepair. A cracked wooden bowl lay before him. With his body still acting on its own, Shan Wu walked across the plaza to stand in front of the filthy boy. As he approached, the boy lowered his head out of respect.

'Seems times are hard,' Shan Wu said.

'The ways of the Tao are difficult to comprehend,' the beggar replied. He raised his bowl, head still lowered and eyes on the ground. Shan Wu saw that the beggar had lost one of his hands at the wrist. He could not explain why, but his heart had begun to race. That voice…

The boy raised his head but did not look Shan Wu in the eye. His hair hung limply across his forehead. The boy smiled ruefully, revealing a tooth that jutted out of his gums at an odd angle. A shock ran through Shan Wu. He knew that twisted tooth. Lying in the dirt in front of him was Gong Wei, Gong Liu's son! Shan Wu felt that he had known all along he would meet Gong Wei; that ever since leaving his room that morning, he was being led for a purpose, taken to this very spot.

Somehow Gong Wei did not yet recognise him. 'We are ever reliant upon the kindness of others,' Gong Wei said.

Time seemed to come to a sudden stop. Memories tugged at Shan Wu, transporting him back to the village. He was standing on the threshold of the hut. Outside, the sunlight made the fields glow. He saw the villagers working, their scarves around their heads to absorb the sweat of their labour. He heard their singing. The crop had been planted and people were full of hope. Father and Mother were out working, and Shan Tuo was walking to the river to get water.

Time jumped ahead. It was early autumn, and the light had begun to fade. Father had entered the hut, had come straight over, bringing his cupped hands to Shan Mu and Gong Wei. Father had smiled broadly. His eyes on the boys, he had opened his hands part way. A chirp erupted from within. 'Hear him sing,' Father had said. 'How lucky!' The boys had gasped as a chirping cricket was passed into their hands.

Shan Wu looked at the filthy beggar seated at his feet. A wave of emotions flooded through him, threatening to choke him. Finally, he found his voice. 'What path led you here?'

Gong Wei wearily leaned his head back against the wall behind him. 'The village I came from was plundered every harvest by a wealthy landlord, a devil with a heart of ice called Baojun. We worked to provide him with the rice he asked for, but every year he asked for more. One day, his retainers came. They took all our winter stores.'

'Why didn't you fight back?' Shan Wu asked.

Gong Wei answered, his voice low, 'We were not warriors, just poor farmers.'

'And what happened after Baojun's retainers took the winter stores?'

'We starved!' Gong Wei cried, a flash of anger raising his voice. But the words had barely escaped when he cringed and lowered his eyes once again. 'Forgive me, sir.'

The memory of Baojun's men riding into the village, the murder of his father, the stealing of the winter stores rose up in front of Shan Wu's eyes. 'Tell me what happened afterwards,' Shan Wu said.

Gong Wei was silent for a few moments. 'My father, Gong Liu, was the head villager. He was the first to die.'

'What of the others?' Shan Wu cried, his throat tight. 'What happened to them?'

'Most of the villagers died—'

'What of Shan Tuo? What happened to him?'

Gong Wei looked up in amazement. He caught Shan Wu's eye for the first time, and a smile of recognition spread quickly across his face. 'Shan Mu!' he said. 'Can it be true? Is it really you?'

'What of Shan Tuo?' Shan Wu repeated through clenched teeth. The thoughts of Gong Wei were clear to Shan Wu. But he had to hear Gong Wei say it. To make what had happened to Shan Tuo impossible to deny, he had to hear the words…

The smile on Gong Wei's face evaporated and once again his eyes dropped to the ground. 'Forgive me. Men came. They took those of us who were still alive, including Shan Tuo. They left you for dead because of your fever. We were taken out of the valley and sold as slaves.' Gong Wei raised his stump. 'My owner cut off my hand – all the better for begging, he told me. The last time I saw Shan Tuo was here in Khotan. He was sold to another trader.'

'When?'

'Three weeks ago.'

'His name?' Shan Wu cried.

Gong Wei shook his head. 'I do not know.'

'Those who sold him – their names!'

'I do not know. I am sorry.'

Shan Wu stepped forward, ready to drive his clenched fists into Gong Wei's bony body. But then he saw his mother's face – as she stood, resting briefly in the near fields – as clearly as if she were there in front of him. As if time were a horse that he could ride faster, the memories of Mother raced ahead. He watched as she grew weaker, as the light left her eyes until she was sick and dying on the floor, until she was dead and cold.

He eyed Gong Wei. 'If only I had come to Khotan sooner. If only I had known.' But Shan Tuo was still alive. There was still hope. Shan Wu dropped ten *wen* into Gong Wei's bowl. They rattled the bowl and leaped around before Gong Wei smothered them with his hand.

'Find out more,' Shan Wu told him. 'Find Shan Tuo!'

Gong Wei looked at the *wen* in his bowl.

'Help me and your bowl will be filled twenty times over. That I promise.'

# CHAPTER 38

—

The next evening, there was a light tapping on his door. Shan Wu opened it and found the owner of the *caravanserai*, Mizben, waiting there.

Mizben bowed deeply. 'Forgive me for disturbing you, but there is someone here to see you.'

Shan Wu's heart leaped. 'Is it a beggar?'

Mizben's expression asked why he had been asked such a strange question, though his lips did not.

Shan Wu's shoulders crumpled. 'Send him away! I do not wish to speak to anyone at present.'

'Yes, sir,' Mizben said and left. But a few moments later, he was back again. 'The gentleman is very insistent, sir. He wants very much to speak with you and has asked me to tell you he has a map that may interest you greatly.'

'I see,' Shan Wu said. 'Very well, send him in.'

The man who entered the room had a smile that spread across his very round face and stuck out from under a giant moustache. He had a black beard that reached down to his belt. He was dressed in fine indigo silks and wore gold hoops around his wrists and expansive waist. A gold ring with a gemstone adorned each of his fingers. He was followed by a man who barely fit through the door. He wore a large tunic of black satin embroidered with gold thread.

'My name is Ochlik,' he said. 'And this is my servant, Mem.'

Mem gave the slightest of nods. Shan Wu noted Mem's powerful neck and broad shoulders.

Ochlik and Shan Wu bowed to one another. Shan Wu offered him a seat and sat down opposite. Mem, more than a head taller than Shan Wu, stood off to the side, his huge arms folded across his chest.

'What can I do for you, sir?' Shan Wu asked. This man, Ochlik, was different to the others who had sought Shan Wu's help since he had arrived in Khotan. The others had mostly been Sogdian traders wishing to know who would pay the most for their goods, or what their prospects were for a safe passage to their destination. And most of them had been poor. But Ochlik oozed wealth from every pore of his body. That wasn't all. The biggest difference was that he, Shan Wu, could not read Ochlik's thoughts. Every time he tried, and he had tried repeatedly, a blinding wall of white light forced him to retreat.

Ochlik smiled.

'What can you do for me...' he said, almost to himself. His piercing hazel eyes fixed themselves on Shan Wu's face. 'I have had men watching you, Shan Wu, ever since I was alerted to your presence in the bazaar. You have not been here long... four, five weeks, I believe?'

Shan Wu nodded. 'About that.'

'And already your name reaches across the city to me.' Ochlik's eyes continued to size up Shan Wu. 'All the same, I was expecting someone more... imposing.'

Shan Wu gave a thin smile. 'You should speak to Ahmed. He deals with any requests for my help.'

'Ah yes. Ahmed. Quite a – what shall I say? – meddlesome little man. He made some demands that I thought rather unrealistic.' Ochlik shrugged and looked at Mem. Mem drew an imaginary dagger across his throat. The meaning was clear; Ahmed would not be joining them. Ever.

Shan Wu willed his face to remain as still as a statue's. Ahmed had saved his life! Ahmed's quick thinking had earned money. Ahmed had also brought him to Khotan, closer to Shan Tuo. He owed him much. But even as his heart pounded harder, his mind was racing on, moving in a different direction... Was it not true that Ahmed had served his purpose? Was it not true he had barely known Ahmed? Was it not true that feeling anger about Ahmed's death was the act of a sentimental child?

'Little would be gained by letting a single death cloud my judgement,' he eventually said.

The hint of a smile played on Ochlik's plump lips. He nodded slowly. 'Then I have a job for you... But first,' he said, offering a smile without humour, 'a test – if that meets with your approval.'

'Very well,' Shan Wu replied. 'Though I am disappointed you feel the need to test me.'

'Indulge me, please,' Ochlik said, clasping his hands together in a pyramid in front of him. Rising, he beckoned Shan Wu to the window. 'If you would be so kind?'

Shan Wu joined him.

'Do you see that tower there?' Ochlik said, pointing across the dark city streets to a pale tower in the near distance. 'That is my home. You are to tell me what image hangs above my bed.' He looked at the table where a small candle flickered. 'Before this flame goes out.'

'And if I do?' Shan Wu asked calmly.

Ochlik snapped his fingers and Mem produced a bag full of gold coins. 'This will be your reward.'

Shan Wu took the bag. He laughed coldly to himself. What a fool the man was!

Ochlik continued to smile at him, but a steely look had entered his eyes. 'I take it you appreciate my generosity?'

Shan Wu placed the bag on the table next to the candle. 'I accept,' he said, 'but on the condition that you wait outside.'

Ochlik bowed and walked out the door with Mem following behind. Shan Wu waited until they had gone, then sat cross-legged upon his bed. He focused intently upon the image of the tower for a moment and then emptied his mind. His spirit rose from his body like mist rising off a lake. After a moment, the sky cleared around him, revealing the constellations above. He willed his spirit towards the tower, across the city, and into the open window closest to the stars. A large bed filled the room, covered by a canopy strung with silk. Above the bed, a golden peacock spread wings studded with turquoise and other precious gems.

In a flash, he was back in his room.

Shan Wu picked up the burning candle and joined them in the carriage waiting outside.

'I can think of no image more fitting for you than a golden peacock,' he said.

Ochlik's smile, which seemed like it could not grow wider, grew wider still. 'You will join us for a meal, yes? I have a business offer for you, such that requires your special talents.'

Ochlik made room for Shan Wu in the carriage and they set off. They rode through the narrow streets, past weavers, coppersmiths and potters, until finally they reached a large arch. Ochlik shouted out a command and the carriage was lowered. Once he had stepped out himself, he asked Shan Wu to follow.

They entered an enormous courtyard ringed with columns. In its centre, a large fountain sprayed water, gushing so much that it spilled over the sides of the basin. Beside it was a roaring fire, a lamb mounted on a rack roasting over it. They sat at a table piled high with dates, figs, a variety of fruits that Shan Wu had never seen before.

Ochlik clapped his hands. 'Let us have music! And dance!' he said to the woman who came over.

A stool, cushioned and draped in embroidered cloth, was placed next to one of the columns. Two men in long white robes came into the room, one carrying a stringed instrument with an ivory carving over the sound hole. He sat on the chair and, tilting his head, began tuning his instrument. The other man was carrying an hourglass-shaped drum made of silver. Its surface was engraved with a dense pattern of flowers and birds. A third man came in, a tambourine in hand. The man with the oud signalled to the others that he was finished tuning. The drummer started, *dum tek tek dum tek*, the sound echoing off the marble stone. The tambourine shimmered out a complementary rhythm, the oud tracing a tune that seemed both mournful and joyous. After a few minutes, a woman emerged from behind the musicians. Wrapped around her upper body were pink and purple scarves made of silk. A purple skirt clung to her swaying hips. Her arms were decorated with flowers painted in henna.

Shan Wu watched as the woman found the rhythm in her body, and directed it to her waist. Gold bells hung from her sash, tinkling with every step she took, keeping time as she moved to the music. He listened to the song the bells were singing, looked back into her eyes, which locked on to his and would not let go.

Ochlik stopped smiling and gestured for Shan Wu to draw nearer. 'I have heard tell of an elixir,' he said in a voice that was only just audible above the music in the room. 'I am willing to pay more than you can imagine.'

When Shan Wu heard the word 'elixir' his body tensed. Could it be…? He stared at Ochlik.

'As you can see,' Ochlik continued, oblivious to the effect the word had had on his acquaintance and waving his hand at the courtyard, 'I do not suffer from a shortage of things to please me. In fact, I do not suffer from anything.' At this, he laughed so hard his belly jiggled.

For what seemed like an aeon, Shan Wu waited for Ochlik's laughter to end.

Wiping his eyes, Ochlik grew serious. 'But there is one thing I want, one thing that you can help me obtain.'

He called Mem to his side and said, 'I wish to be alone with our friend, Mem. Please make sure we are not disturbed.'

Mem pulled out Ochlik's chair for him. Shan Wu followed Mem and Ochlik down a series of halls. Ochlik took a great key from his waist and ushered Shan Wu into a large room with a high stone ceiling. Mem followed and closed the heavy door behind them. He stood in the doorway, arms crossed, legs spread wide like a statue. The room, half as large as the courtyard, was lavishly furnished. The walls were hung with colourful tapestries, the floors lined with shimmering silk carpets. Light shone through golden globes suspended from the ceiling with holes pierced in their sides. These created a great shower of light, which was amplified by the reflections off the other gold objects that lay on the tables and hung from the walls.

'Please,' Ochlik said and directed Shan Wu to a chair. 'I have something to show you.'

He walked to a large, heavily bound chest in the corner of the room. From around his neck, he took a key, fitted it into the lock, and opened the chest. He brought a scroll over to Shan Wu. He clasped the scroll in both hands. 'Indeed, I have spent more than a decade trying to find it. And equally as long trying to find someone able to help me make use of it.'

He looked at Shan Wu and his eyes burned. 'Consider yourself most fortunate.' He unrolled the scroll and set it on the table. 'You see before you the Neijing Tu.'

# CHAPTER 39

—

The Neijing Tu. Shan Wu devoured it with his eyes. And yet… wasn't it rather small? He recalled listening to his grandmother's tales of the legendary map, only half-believing them. He had imagined a great scroll, a sweeping, vast portrayal of the heavens. Instead, the square-shaped map was of a modest size – about that of a large book, perhaps.

'It's smaller than I expected,' Shan Wu said. Was it really the Neijing Tu? How could such a small map guide a person to the Jade Palace, home of the Immortals?

Ochlik gave a knowing smile. 'Pick it up,' he said.

Pinching it at its edges, Shan Wu did so. He gasped. As though floating in air, everything on the map – its fields, which lay at the bottom, its mountains at the top, its writing – swelled and shrank, and, pulsating gently, changed position.

Ochlik chortled. 'Whichever way you turn, it does not matter. The Neijing Tu will always point towards the Jade Palace.'

Shan Wu turned left and right. The map's icons spun and realigned with each turn. Shan Wu laughed. It was like nothing he had ever seen. Standing stationary, he ran his eyes over the map, following a path from bottom to top, passing people riding a carriage, a gate, a man ploughing the fields with a water buffalo, linked yin-yang symbols, a woman weaving in an orchard. Nearing the map's top edge, he passed a twelve-storied pagoda. And at the very top, nestled among the peaks of a mountain range shrouded in clouds, his eyes came to rest on an exquisite, pulsating ink drawing of a fountain whose boundaries expanded and contracted like a heart. Shan Wu read the characters written next to it: *Eyebrows of white-headed Lao-tzu hanging down to earth.*

'The Jade Palace. Home of the Immortals,' Shan Wu whispered.

'And the home of The Elixir of Immortality,' Ochlik said, reaching into the chest and withdrawing a large gourd, a golden peacock with emerald tail-feathers covering its surface. 'You will fill this with the elixir and return here. Then I will drink it in front of your eyes. I have read that it tastes purer than the purest water.'

'Why do you not go yourself?' Shan Wu asked.

'To the Jade Palace?' Ochlik smiled. 'I have middling powers – sufficient to stop you reading my mind and to control the minds of imbeciles, but insufficient to undertake a journey there.'

'I could take the Neijing Tu, go to the palace, drink the elixir while I am there, then disappear when I return to the world of things.'

'You could do that.' Ochlik said, 'but I believe you will return to bring me the elixir.' He held his hand out, indicating with a lazy gesture the room's burnished statuettes, thick tapestries, carved furniture. 'Tell me, what would you have as your own?'

The question struck Shan Wu with sudden force. *What would he have?* The answer was not long in coming. What single desire had burned in his heart since the day Baojun's men came and stole his family from him? Yes, he would bring the elixir for Ochlik. Then he would pursue the retainers – not just the one who had killed his father, but *all* of them. But he would need more than just time.

'My weight in gold,' he said simply.

For a moment, Ochlik's hard eyes burrowed into Shan Wu's, but then he gave a shrug. 'As you wish. But there is one other thing. I do not think the Immortals are eager to give their elixir away.' He went to a corner of the room and pulled out a broad sword in a heavy scabbard. It, too, was encrusted in gems.

'I will have no need of that,' Shan Wu answered.

'I can only assume you know what is best,' Ochlik said. 'But be warned – I have given my life to acquiring the elixir. I will not be very tolerant of failure.'

Shan Wu returned his look with a grim smile. 'Give me three days. I will bring back the elixir.'

'Good.' He turned to Mem, a wide smile across his face once more. 'We will be waiting. Won't we, Mem?'

Mem nodded, his eyes on Shan Wu, hard and cold.

Shan Wu turned to go.

'Three days,' Ochlik said.

When Shan Wu stepped out of Ochlik's house and back onto the streets, he was carrying the gourd and the Neijing Tu. Ochlik wanted the Elixir of Immortality. He, Shan Wu, would go to the Jade Palace and get it. Ochlik would pay the promised gold and he would use the money to find mercenaries, pay them to kill Baojun's retainers and wipe out every one of their relatives – even if it took several of his lifetimes.

He realised he was smiling broadly. Why not? Everywhere around him were sights he had been blind to before, sounds that had gone unheard. He smelled a chicken cooking, the aroma of its spices – sesame, garlic, soy sauce – from a kitchen three blocks away. As he walked, his stomach rumbled. The food smelled wonderful. But more delicious was the prospect of having the retainer who had killed his father tied to a tree while he watched his children's throats being slit, one by one. Another thought occurred to him. If he delivered the elixir to Ochlik, he would be rich, rich enough to pay others to help him sweep the country in search of his brother.

'Spare some change.' The voice came from a beggar sitting propped against the wall of Shan Wu's lodgings. The beggar's face was etched with lines as deep as valleys. His withered hand reached up, palm open. Shan Wu knocked it away.

Tomorrow, he would speak to Gong Wei again, ask if he had any further information. Perhaps he would also go to the market, speak to some of the traders there. Someone, somewhere, had the information he wanted. Whether they were prepared to tell him or not, he would find out. He would read every mind in Khotan if he had to!

'I will find you, little brother,' he said, opening the door to his lodgings and stepping inside. 'I swear it.'

Shan Wu hung the gourd by its leather strap around his shoulder and across his chest. Gripping the Neijing Tu, he wetted the fingers of his other hand, reached over, and snuffed out the candle next to his bedside. The air was brightening, the dawn approaching. It was time.

Lying down once again, he breathed slowly. Moments later, he was in the world beyond. Once again, the air was riven with dark veins running like black rivers. But this time the horizon glowed a faint, pervasive green. And he had the Neijing Tu. It lay in his hands, its drawings and characters glowing as if they had been written by a brush dipped in fire. Brighter and brighter in the grey, smoky air they shone so that his view of them grew clearer, more defined.

Shan Wu pointed the map towards the horizon. The map's contents shifted as he moved. He smiled as he caught his first glimpse of the Jade Palace.

# CHAPTER 40

▬

Shan Wu crested the top of the hill and was suddenly enveloped in a thick mist. Unable to see, he continued forward. The mist gave way slowly, revealing a giant square, its four corners marked by pillars. Two rivers flowed on either side of the palace, gushing torrents that made the palace complex look like a giant tortoise coming to the surface of a great sea. A long bridge spanned from the immense courtyard in front of him to the mountains on either side. Square stones were set in the ground, creating a thoroughfare so broad, four carriages could ride in side by side. The bridge was lined with low fences, painted in bright blues and reds. As he approached the palace, he saw a flight of steps set in tiers, so that the palace itself sat upon a platform. Four columns, each twice as thick as a man's body, supported a series of square arches, the middle gate spanning many metres above the heads of those who passed beneath. These were decorated with flowers in greens, blues, yellows. Red paper lanterns, the size of huge barrels, hung from the wooden beams, glowing bright.

The building that lay behind the gate was three times as wide again, topped with roof tiles that gently curved up at the corners like leaves reaching for sunlight. Atop each of these roofs were golden dragons, a pair on either side, their mouths gaping.

Above the main entrance was a dragon made entirely of jade, large enough to swallow a human whole. It had large whiskers, a flowing beard and a body covered with plated scales. Tian Lan had told him many things as they had walked together, of the world of things and the world beyond. Here was one of the Si Shou, the celestial guardians. *Were it not for my mission,* Shan Wu thought, *this dragon would be a symbol of good fortune.* But its sharp teeth and claws would not be good fortune for anyone who had to face it. Would all he had learned from Tian Lan be enough to stop it from ripping him to pieces?

He was standing between a pair of statues carved entirely from jade. Each was twice his size. These lion guardians, *shishi*, were powerful protectors, controlled by the harnesses and bells around their massive necks. One was leaning his paw on a ball, the other pinning a lion cub down on its back.

The palace felt more solid than any building he had felt down below. It was a massive place that seemed to have been carved from a single piece of wood. Shan Wu willed his spirit up and was able to get a view of the entire grounds. The building was in the shape of a square as well, with large halls at each of its corners. Shan Wu wondered if it housed anyone other than the Immortals – surely it was too large for eight, no matter how much room they needed. He had never before seen anything like it – a collection of buildings as elegant and balanced as a giant mandala.

He recalled the map. There it was, the Eastern Hall – resting spot of the elixir. He realised that his spirit, hovering in the air, was exposed and came back to the ground for fear of being seen.

Shan Wu landed on the ground lightly just outside the Eastern Hall and quickly hid himself in the shadows. He looked out from behind one of the pillars, scanning for anyone, anything at all. He appeared to be alone; nothing stood between him and the entrance to the hall.

Shan Wu crossed the square to the Eastern Hall, watching all the while for any movement, any sign that he was being followed. It was quiet but for the sound of a flute far in the distance.

He stepped forward and heard a sharp click. He froze. It was the echo of his footstep on the stone. He removed his shoes and approached the giant door as quietly as he could. The images of two gods stared down at him, facing each other at either side of the entrance. These had been put in place to keep evil spirits from entering. They had long hair, moustaches and beards, wore brightly coloured flowing robes and carried large axes. Their fierce faces made him pause. Dare he enter? He felt fear grip his belly. Would they bar him from going inside? What would he do if the other guardians that Tian Lan had told him about – the Red Phoenix, the White Tiger – stopped him? Where were they? For a moment, he stood as still as a rock, fearing they would appear.

But then he laughed to himself and, relaxing his hunched shoulders, he stood as tall and straight as he could. Fear – what use had he for fear? Had he not already suffered cold, hunger, burning heat? And was he not the greatest shaman of the age?

No, he was not afraid.

# CHAPTER 41

━

But still, he was surprised at how easily he'd got in. Perhaps the Immortals never had any fear. Why would they? Perhaps this was his destiny, to claim the power he had been born to hold and wield forever.

A gentle breeze wafted through the palace. All was quiet.

The Elixir of Immortality flowed from a fountain into a deep basin in the courtyard. Shan Wu looked into the basin, into the purest water in all of creation. He looked at his reflection, at the shape of his face, his piercing eyes, his narrow chin, his high cheekbones. *After drinking, I will be like this – forever,* he thought. *Time will move on, mountains will rise and fall. I will remain unchanged.*

Shan Wu cupped his hands and dipped them into the elixir. It felt like he was bathing his hands in sunlight. He slowly raised the liquid to his lips and felt the warmth slide down his throat, coating it in a glow. The energy spread through his chest as the elixir was drawn into his blood, glowing brighter as it was absorbed by each of his cells. The warm tingle moved outward, through his arms until it reached his fingertips, down through his legs and feet. Every one of his senses felt sharper, his muscles flexing with newfound power.

All Shan Wu's doubts were gone, replaced by a clarity he'd never known before. A loud noise surprised him and he turned. There it was again. He looked to find where the noise was coming from and realised to his amazement that it was the call of a bird of paradise. Yet it was not the bird itself that surprised him. The bird was perched on a tree branch across a wide valley. Despite the distance, his eyes could see the smallest details on the bird's feathers. He could count the scales on its feet if he wished. The Jade Palace shimmered before his eyes, became more solid, more real.

Shan Wu drank till he could drink no more. He filled the gourd and placed the stopper back on. He scanned the courtyard for any presence, but all he could hear was the rushing of the rivers that bounded the palace. Placing his shoes back on, Shan Wu retraced his path. As he exited the gate, he looked over his shoulder at the dragon lying above the doorway. How foolish he'd been to worry!

He returned to his body and found himself once again in his room. Carrying the gourd, he stepped out into the streets and made his way into Ochlik's palace. His senses were alive in a way they had never been before, the vibrancy of the sights and sounds of the city magnified a thousand times. In the courtyard, some musicians were playing. He sat down, enjoying the interplay of drummers and the rhythms of the dancers' feet. Within a few seconds, Mem appeared at his side. He did not say a word but escorted him to Ochlik's chamber. In the grand room, Ochlik was seated, surrounded by a mountain of cushions. When he saw the gourd in Shan Wu's hands, he struggled to his feet as quickly as he could. Behind them, Mem stood, guarding the door.

'So you have returned. Successful, I hope.' Ochlik bobbed about nervously, his eyes shining, beside himself to have the gourd in his hands.

'Oh yes, I have been successful – more so than I could have imagined. But…' He paused, watching in amusement as Ochlik's agitation grew. 'I have changed my mind,' Shan Wu said. 'You will double the fee you promised.' He looked at the gourd again, then turned to face Ochlik. 'No. Triple.'

Ochlik's face grew purple with rage. 'Mem, seize him!' he screamed.

Mem snarled and his giant hands grabbed Shan Wu's throat. But they closed on thin air. Shan Wu had vanished. So had the gourd.

Shan Wu was dragged across the thin line separating the two worlds. In an instant, he was back – back at the Jade Palace.

'What is the meaning of this?'

The voice of the questioner boomed in the courtyard, echoing and recasting itself five or six times. Shan Wu searched left and right. Where had it come from? Who had said it?

Suddenly, a hand tightly gripped his shoulder. He turned to see one of the Immortals, Li Tieguai. He was leaning on an iron crutch and wearing a gold hoop around his head. Shan Wu knew that Li Tieguai had gained immortality only to have his spirit inhabit the body of a lame beggar, but Li Tieguai was even uglier than Shan Wu had expected.

Standing around Shan Wu, materialising from the emptiness, other Immortals appeared. It was as if they had been watching him all along. He counted six of them.

'How dare you come to our home,' Li Tieguai said. 'How dare you steal that which belongs to us alone!'

Shan Wu's voice was barely a whisper in comparison. 'My name is Shan Wu. I am a shaman in the Northern Kingdom. I have travelled long to reach you and—'

'We know of you, Shan Wu. You think too highly of yourself, mortal.' This came from Zhongli Quan, whose dark expression spoke of the anger he felt – it was his elixir Shan Wu had stolen. 'You play with forces that are far more powerful than you can imagine!' he roared, his bare belly quivering.

Shan Wu turned to face Lu Dongbin, the scholar. *There is little doubt that he will see that I, too, am powerful,* he thought.

'Surely you, Lu Dongbin, with your profound understanding of alchemy, recognise the truth of my claim to be seen as one of you. You have seen the depths of my knowledge; my travels in the world beyond; my reading of others' minds.'

Lu Dongbin looked down at Shan Wu and shook his head. 'The wise man does not bend nature but follows where she leads until he sees his path as one and the same.' He almost seemed disappointed. 'You would do better to control yourself.'

'Your pride has brought you here in error,' said a young man, who Shan Wu guessed by his flute must be Han Xiang Zi.

'Error?' Shan Wu cried, the anger rising in his throat like bile. 'I now see how foolish I have been. You stand before me, casting judgement as if I were unworthy to raise my eyes. Yes, I am a fool – a fool to plead with you, asking you to accept me as an equal. An equal! Now that I, too, am immortal, I will not beg for your approval! I am greater than any of you!'

Shan Wu began chanting, his feet tracing patterns as his hand waved around him, creating a protective sphere. The air around Shan Wu began to hum, shimmer. He summoned all of his power, focusing it upon his palms, which were pressed together in front of his face. They glowed, an iridescent rainbow of colours. There was a great crackling and an arc of pure energy burst forth, searing a path through the air to slam against Li Tieguai's chest. The force of the blast threw Li Tieguai in the air, his misshapen body hitting the ground several heartbeats after his iron crutch. He rolled over, groaned piteously, and was still. The silver medallion round his neck lay beside him, broken into three jagged shards.

Lu Dongbin, face flushed with rage and eyes on fire, roared and unsheathed his broadsword. 'Enough!' he bellowed. He pointed his sword at Shan Wu.

Shan Wu tried to raise his hands to defend himself, but his hands would not move. His entire body was frozen as if encased in ice. A terror he'd never felt before began to creep up his spine.

One of the Immortals stepped forward. Dressed in a red uniform and a tall, angular hat, he raised a jade tablet in front of him and said in a cold voice, 'I, Cao Guojiu, speaker for we Eight Immortals, pass sentence upon you. For your theft of the Elixir of Immortality, for your abuse of powers and attempt to disrupt the Tao, for your presumption that you are equal to the Immortals and your actions against us, you will be imprisoned for time immemorial unless the Immortals, in their mercy, decide otherwise.'

Then Zhang Guolao stepped forward. His wispy, grey hair fluttered like butterflies. From the sleeve of his robe, he produced a small, jade ball. He held it out in the palm of his hand. Shan Wu could see it was a puzzle ball – jade dragons carved on its outer surface enclosed other surfaces, more and yet more dragons, their intricate walls tightening towards a dark centre. The old man began muttering words that Shan Wu had never heard before, but whose purpose he could guess…

'No, please,' Shan Wu cried. He watched as Zhang Guolao's lips continued to move. Desperate, Shan Wu looked from one Immortal's face to another, pleading, begging them to reconsider. Their hard eyes said their decision was made.

Shan Wu knelt, clasping his hands together. 'What of my brother?' he cried. 'What happened to Shan Tuo? Tell me, I beg you.'

A dizzying green light flashed from Lu Dongbin's sword and a searing pain shot through Shan Wu's body. The Neijing Tu dropped from Shan Wu's hand. Mouth open, Shan Wu stared. Like a stream composed of a million, million tiny ants, pieces of his fingers, his hands, his arms were slowly detaching themselves from his body and flying through the air towards the jade ball.

'No!' Shan Wu screamed, seeing a vision of the years he would be imprisoned in the jade ball – of the loneliness, of the darkness he would endure. 'You can't do this! You can't!' But the Immortals' faces remained unchanged.

Finally, all hope gone, his fate sealed, Shan Wu stood and sneered. 'I'll destroy you!' he said, spitting the venomous words. 'I'll destroy you – you and your pathetic, grovelling followers. One day, you'll see. One day, all humanity will pay. One day…' Shan Wu stopped and his eyes bulged as he saw pieces of his lips detach themselves from his mouth, the jade ball dragging them towards itself. He gave a strangulated cry. A moment later, his mouth, followed by his face, his head, neck and shoulders followed the rest of his body until he was inside his jade prison, caught in the unbreakable clutches of its carved dragons.

Once inside the dragonball, Shan Wu felt himself being carried, and a moment later, dropped. For ages the dragonball turned and twisted, weightlessly falling through the air, until water was all around it. Then there was a final glimpse of the sky for Shan Wu before the dragonball plunged below the surface of the sea and began to sink. By infinite shades, blue turned to indigo turned to black as the dragonball dropped deeper and deeper. Finally, when the dragonball settled with a soft bump on the ocean floor, Shan Wu could see nothing. It was as if the Immortals had plucked out his eyes. And though he knew no one would hear, though he did not wish to give voice to the desolation he felt, he could not stop the scream, long and loud, that escaped from his mouth.

He was trapped at the centre of the jade dragonball in a darkness without end.

Sword at his side, Lu Dongbin reached down and picked up the Neijing Tu. 'This will be needed,' he said simply, rolling the map and tying it with a tapering ribbon of silk.

# PART 6

# FORT WILLIAM,
# SCOTLAND
## THE PRESENT DAY

# Chapter 42

—

'Sara, we're almost there. Sara?'

Her mother's voice above the hum of the car's tyres on the rough tarmac road interrupted her dream. For a moment, she was listening to the voice and at the same time traipsing down the longest corridor imaginable, her feet buried in white, fluffy clouds, mirrors on the corridor's walls glistening far into the distance. 'Hmm,' Sara said, eyes still glued together.

'We're almost at Fort William, Sara,' her mother said gently.

'Okay,' Sara replied, eyes still shut. 'Just a few more minutes…' She was so tired, she was slurring her words. She didn't care. Another wave of delicious sleepiness swept over her.

'There she be!' yelled her father.

'Dad, *please*!'

'We'll be there in a few minutes,' her mum said, more firmly this time.

'I didn't sleep in the plane,' Sara said grumpily.

'Isn't she beautiful?' her father yelled. 'And not a cloud in sight. Look at that!'

Sara could guess what her father was getting so excited about. Slowly, she raised her head off the rental car's back seat, but she didn't want to open her eyes just yet. It had been midnight when she, her mother and her father had left Beijing. The airport had been busy with lots of other families of school-aged kids leaving for the summer holidays. Despite the crowds, the plane had taken off on time, its engines roaring as they thrust Beijing Capital International airport and the Chaoyang District behind them, then gently thrumming as they raised the plane higher and higher into the night.

At first, Sara had been quite sure she would sleep on the flight. She had watched a movie and had begun to watch another when the meal arrived. After that, when the cabin lights had been dimmed, she had popped in ear buds and listened to some music by Martin Fröst. The cabin seat had been soft, the music had been good, the temperature had been fine. But no matter what, she hadn't been able to fall asleep. Finally, she had given up, gazing out of the window as China, Kyrgyzstan, Uzbekistan and others – their cities like a patchwork of beacons – slipped past. To Sara, it felt like she had seen every one of them, and that she had seen at least some of the old Silk Road's four thousand miles pass beneath her.

When they arrived in London, the sun was fully above the horizon. Usually, Sara liked mornings. Usually, she was the first person awake in her apartment in Beijing. But not this time. All she wanted to do was wrap herself in a blanket and snooze.

'Come on, Sleeping Beauty,' her father said, laying a hand on her shoulder as they waited to disembark the plane and enter the terminal. 'It won't be long now till you are in the bonniest wee toon in the Highlands.'

Sara was too tired to laugh at her father's exaggerated Scottish accent. She sighed. If there was anything worse than feeling tired, it was feeling tired when someone else was full of energy. Why couldn't she have slept like her father always did on flights, like a hibernating bear?

Another flight, just an hour this time, from Heathrow to Glasgow took them to Scotland where her father hired a rental car and began the drive to Fort William. The last thing Sara remembered before she fell asleep was crossing the River Clyde on a bridge

– Erskine, she thought its name was – and her father telling her that the shipbuilders along the river had built the *Cutty Sark*, the *Queen Mary*, and the *QE2*. Sara sort of knew that the *QE2* was an ocean liner but had no idea about the *Cutty Sark*. She hadn't had time to ask before she fell asleep.

Sara rubbed her eyes now and finally opened them. She ran her fingers through her hair. 'How long did I sleep?' she asked, stretching.

'A few hours. Are you feeling better?' her mother asked.

Sara nodded. Her hair was a mess! She pulled it quickly into a ponytail and tied it with a band. It would do for now. Her father was leaning forward at the steering wheel, staring through the windscreen with a huge grin on his face. It was infectious. Excitement tingled through her.

'What a view,' he whispered.

And it was. In front of them, like a giant's shoulder, the mountain rose above Fort William to a cloudless, rounded peak. Because they were approaching from the south, Sara couldn't see the cliffs on the north side, but they were there – the highest in Britain. The mountain was *huge*. When she had looked at pictures on the net, the mountain had looked less… scary. But now, as they drew ever closer, the mountain seemed to rise up and loom over them and Sara could almost feel the height and weight of it. It felt… Sara struggled to put it into words. It didn't look evil. It looked… unforgiving – even under the blue sky that was brilliantly illuminating the green on its lower slopes. It looked, she decided, like an assassin who did his job with a pleasant smile.

'I'll call Mrs Morton and tell her we are almost there.'

Mrs Morton was the woman at whose bed and breakfast they were staying. Sara had never been in a 'bed and breakfast' before. According to her father, B&Bs were somewhere between private homes and small hotels. People rented out rooms in their house to tourists, usually during the summer, providing them with a place to sleep and breakfast in the morning. Sara had also never been to Scotland before, even though her father was born in Fort William. She had, of course, been to the UK many times to visit her grandmother, but her grandmother had moved away from Scotland soon after the birth of her only son and had lived in London for most of her life. Usually, Sara, her mother and her father stayed in London with her grandmother during the summer holidays. but this trip was different. This time, her father had promised to take her to the place where he was born. This time, he had promised to take her mountain climbing – because this time, they were going to climb Ben Nevis, the highest mountain in the United Kingdom.

# Chapter 43

—

Sara stepped out of the car and onto a semi-circular gravel driveway. The driveway was part of a large plot of land in which a grey stone house stood surrounded by its own beautiful gardens. A woman, presumably the owner of the house, Mrs Morton, was stepping out of the front door. In a few quick strides she was with them, shaking hands with Sara's father and mother.

'Hello, everyone. Welcome to Loch Linnhe House! My name is Mrs Morton.'

She was a small woman with curly grey hair and a powdered face that was half hidden by large glasses whose thick lenses magnified her eyes. Her nose, Sara thought, looked like a small, sharp beak. Sara tried to stop the word 'owl' popping into her head and failed miserably.

'And you must be Sara,' said Mrs Morton.

'Yes. Nice to meet you,' Sara said, shaking Mrs Morton's hand.

Mrs Morton smiled. 'My, what a lovely-looking young lady you are. What beautiful hair!'

Sara started to blush. She wasn't used to these kinds of compliments. Ignoring the smirk on her father's face as he went past her towards the boot of the car, she pulled her ponytail over her shoulder and mumbled her thanks, not knowing quite what to say.

Mrs Morton smiled. 'And tall for your age.'

Sara didn't know what to say to that either. She supposed she was.

'So,' continued Mrs Morton, 'your dad tells me you and he are planning to climb the Ben tomorrow.'

*The Ben?* thought Sara. *What's the Ben?* She glanced at her father. He flicked his eyes towards the mountain. *Oh, right – Ben Nevis!*

'That's right, Mrs Morton,' Sara's mother said, joining her husband at the back of the car and pulling out Sara's case, the smallest of the three. 'We're planning to visit the Glenfinnan viaduct early in the morning – Sara's a big Harry Potter fan. Then we'll come back and my husband and Sara will climb… the Ben.' Her mother handed Sara her case.

Sara smiled at Mrs Morton. Her mother was an even bigger Harry Potter fan than she was! All the same, she was looking forward to seeing the place where the express train from Platform Nine and Three-Quarters swept Harry, Ron, Hermione, and all the rest of them across the valley and on to Hogwarts… but probably not as much as her mum was!

'Well, isn't that nice,' Mrs Morton said, smiling at Sara before she turned back to Sara's mother. 'But you'll know there are roadworks along the A830 – the road from Fort William to Glenfinnan? I just mention it because they'll want to start climbing the Ben sharpish – I mean, before ten in the morning.'

'Actually, we didn't know there were roadworks, Mrs Morton,' said Sara's mother, pulling out Sara's clarinet case and handing it to her. 'Is there a reason why they should start climbing the mountain before ten?'

'The forecast says there'll be rain in the afternoon. Better to get up the Ben early so you get a view from the top.'

'How long does it usually take to climb the mountain?' Sara asked.

Mrs Morton's face crinkled. 'It depends how fast you walk, my dear. But usually it takes about six hours.'

Sara thought she had misheard. 'Did you say six hours?' she asked, glaring at her father, who had pulled the last remaining suitcase from the car. He raised his eyebrows as if to say, 'Well, what did you expect?'

Six hours! Why hadn't she asked that question before she agreed to climb the Ben?

Sara had the feeling once again that the mountain was looming over her. She dared not look in its direction. The fact was that every time she did, a shiver of cold fear went through her body.

Mrs Morton's peal of laughter broke the momentary silence.

'Oh, don't worry, you'll be fine. Absolutely fine,' Mrs Morton said, addressing Sara. Then her gaze hardened. 'But just make sure you give the Ben a proper sacrifice… You don't want the mountain to be angry with you, do you now?'

Sara froze. She shot her father a puzzled look. 'Sacrifice…?'

Before her father could say anything, Mrs Morton let another peal of laughter fill the late afternoon air. 'Oh my! I *am* a wicked old woman!' she said, wiping away a mirthful tear from the corner of her eye. 'I'm just pulling your leg, my dear. Don't listen to me!'

Sara's father laughed and locked the boot. Sara's mother looked less happy.

'Ready?' Mrs Morton asked.

'Ready,' replied Sara's father, gripping in each hand a handle of a suitcase.

'If you'd like to follow me,' Mrs Morton said, nodding towards the red front door, 'I'll show you to your rooms. I'm sure you'll want to freshen up after your long drive.'

Sara's father agreed and, struggling with the heavy cases, he and Sara's mother joined Mrs Morton as she led them into Loch Linnhe House.

But Sara didn't move. Ben Nevis was changing. A sudden mist was rolling across its peak, thin at first but growing thicker. As

Sara watched, the mist raced across the mountain and, moments later, Sara was looking at nothing. The mountain had gone, disappeared as though it had never existed, and in its place was a pale, shadowy mist.

Sara shivered. What was the word she wanted to use? She searched her memory… What was the word she'd seen on *Word of the Day*? Of course! 'Sepulchral', meaning 'gloomy, from a tomb'.

The mist covering the Ben was sepulchral.

# CHAPTER 44

━

In warm sunshine, they started to climb the Ben at a place called Achintree. Sara followed her father as he led them along a well-worn mountain track. At first, they were walking on a gentle hillside covered with ferns, heather and grass. The track wasn't steep but high above them Sara could see it grew more scarped and there were fewer ferns, more scree slopes, and more boulders.

'We'll eat our sandwiches at the Halfway Lochan. It's at 570 metres,' Sara's father had said when they left Achintree. Sara had agreed; 570 metres didn't seem that high. But she soon wondered if she'd ever reach it. The track was mostly dirt but all along it there were flat boulders. Sometimes the boulders made small steps, which were easy to climb over, but often they didn't. Often, the steps the boulders made were high, and to get over these, Sara had to strain her thighs, pushing herself off the ground and climbing with her hands just to get on top of them.

Finally, after hours of struggling, Sara was ready to turn back when her father pointed to a small body of water lying in the valley they had climbed into. 'Halfway Lochan,' he had said, throwing off his rucksack and finding a place to sit on the rough heather. 'It's not really halfway, but it's a good place to stop for a bite to eat.'

Sara nodded and collapsed beside her father onto the rough heather. Her thighs were on fire – really aching, really beginning to tremble. 'How much longer to the top?' she asked, happy her voice wasn't shaking as much as her legs. She imagined a helicopter landing, the pilot beckoning, being flown back to Mrs Morton's guesthouse where a warm bath and a soft bed were waiting. She smiled. Lying back in the heather, she stretched her legs. Each of them seemed to weigh a ton.

'A few more hours,' her father replied.

Sara managed not to groan, but only just. She sat up again. Some food would make her feel better. It always did. From her rucksack, she unwrapped a peanut-butter sandwich – one that Mrs Morton had prepared for her that morning – and bit into it, gazing at the Halfway Lochan's dark, almost black water as she chewed. They had started walking later than planned. The roadworks to Glenfinnan, as Mrs Morton said they would, had delayed them, and by the time they had dropped off Sara's mother in the town, driven to Achintree, put on their boots, and started the walk, it was after eleven. 'Will we make it to the top before the mist comes down?' Sara asked.

'If you chew a bit faster,' her father replied.

'Ha ha, very funny.'

Her father's face grew serious. 'So, how are you feeling?' he asked.

Before Sara could answer, a family – all six of them wearing caps with the Italian flag sewn onto them – appeared. One by one, each of them said hello and passed by, swinging their walking poles as they went. Sara watched as the youngest of the group, a girl perhaps two or three years younger than herself, struggled to keep pace with her older siblings. Each time she fell behind, the girl would skip forward and catch them up. Sara sighed. Over the last few big boulders, her legs had begun to wobble as though all the strength in them had leaked out. She hadn't expected the climb to be easy, but she hadn't expected it to be this difficult either. She was seriously doubting her chances of getting to the top – she had never felt so tired in her life. And yet, for some reason, she wasn't ready to say that; she wasn't ready to accept that the mountain had defeated her. 'I'm okay,' she mumbled, gazing at the Lochan.

'You know, you don't have to continue if you don't want to,' he said gently. 'We can always come back another time and try again.'

Sara stared at the great cotton wool clouds floating in the deeply blue sky. It was hard to believe that the weather was about to change, but far on the horizon, the clouds were greyer. Much greyer. She thought about her father's suggestion. Should they come back another time? The weather was going to turn bad. When it did, they wouldn't be able to see anything from the summit. So what was the point? Why not just come back another time when the weather was better? Sara opened her mouth, but closed it again.

She thought about the clarinet. At first, she had hated it. It was so difficult to play – all those parts: the reed, the barrel, the tone hole rings, the bridge keys, the ligature. Trying to get her fingers to move, to play the notes she wanted to play – it had been so frustrating, and she had wanted to quit *so* many times. But the point was, she hadn't. She had kept going, kept practising, kept getting better. Now she was going to take her ABRSM Grade 6 when she went back to school. She wasn't a great clarinet player – she wasn't even the best in her school – but she had succeeded in becoming better. She opened her mouth… and closed it again. What if it was pride? Was she just too embarrassed to say she couldn't go on? Sara wasn't sure. She felt confused. She decided to change the subject.

'Why did Mrs Morton joke about a sacrifice to the mountain?'

'Actually,' her father said, smiling, 'it's not so silly. Have you heard of Lindow Man?'

Sara shook her head.

'He's one of the famous bog bodies.'

'Bog bodies! What're they?'

'Well, the ancient Celts believed that bogs were sacred places, a connection between Heaven and earth, so they made sacrifices to the gods – *human* sacrifices,' her father said, melodramatically emphasising the word 'human' with a stupid, scary voice.

Sara rolled her eyes.

'Lindow Man is the name of one of the most famous bog bodies,' continued her father. 'He was killed about two thousand years ago. Now you can see him in the British Museum. We should go there when we get back.'

Sara nodded.

'So anyway, it seems like after Lindow Man was fed some bread, he was strangled and hit on the head, then his throat was cut—'

'Ewww…' Sara said.

'—and he was put, face down, into the bog. Some people think the three ways he was killed – bludgeoning, strangulation and throat-cutting – was to honour three separate gods: Tarainis, Esus and Teutates, I think.'

Sara raised her eyebrows.

'I read about them in Loch Linnhe House last night. Thanks to the bats in Mrs Morton's roof, your mother couldn't sleep. And because she couldn't sleep, I couldn't sleep.' Her father looked at her. 'You didn't hear a thing, did you?'

Sara smiled. 'Nope.'

'Lucky you.'

For a moment, Sara and her father were silent, staring up at the mountain track. The next part of the mountain was very different from the one they had just climbed. Now the path zig-zagged across a grey rock. It looked like the surface of the moon.

'You know,' her father said, grin spreading, 'there are two translations of the name Ben Nevis. Some people think it means Mountain of Heaven. But I like the other one better.'

'Okay, what is it?' Sara asked, suspecting it was something corny.

'Malicious Mountain.'

Sara looked at her father. 'Malicious Mountain,' she repeated, thinking about her reaction the day before when the mist had rolled across the Ben's summit as she stood in the Loch Linnhe House driveway. 'Have there been many people killed on the Ben?'

'There are probably one or two deaths every year. A few years back, over 40 people had to be rescued.'

They stared up at the shoulder in front of them. 'Is it my imagination, or is it getting colder?' Sara asked.

'It is colder,' her father replied. 'The clouds are getting darker and the wind's getting a bit stronger.'

A distant peal of laughter interrupted them. It had come from the Italian family, who were now tiny figures in the distance. The sound floated in the air a moment and disappeared. Sara stared up at them. Behind the others in her family, the young girl was still there, still climbing.

'So… upwards?' her father asked, turning to face Sara.

'Upwards,' she replied.

# CHAPTER 45

—

'That's the ruined observatory,' cried Sara's father through the whipping wind and rain that lashed across the summit. He pointed to a gloomy, ruined building in the near distance. Even though it wasn't very far away, Sara could barely see it through the swirling mist. 'We're near the cairn.'

'The what?' Sara shouted, holding on to the hood of her rain jacket with both hands to stop it being ripped from her head, and sheltering as best she could behind her father. 'What's a cairn?'

'It's a pile of stones,' her father yelled. 'It marks the top of the mountain.'

'It's bigger and flatter than I thought,' Sara shouted. 'The summit, I mean.'

'Yeah, it's about the size of two football pitches. We have to be careful: there are gullies on the north side – 600-metre cliffs. Stick close to me, okay?'

'Okay,' replied Sara, following her father as he leaned over and pushed his body into the wind and rain.

Suddenly, a huge gust of wind struck them, making them stagger several steps before they were able to regain their balance. Her father turned. 'Summer in Scotland!' he cried, the words barely reaching Sara before being whipped away by the wind.

Sara grinned and leaning into the blast, they continued. They crossed a small river – her father called it Red Burn stream – and as soon as they did, the sky opened and rain came pouring down. Sara couldn't believe how quickly it happened. They pushed on. Mist was falling. The wind was howling; the rain lashing. When they reached the flat summit, the visibility was reduced to a few metres. Nevertheless, she was loving it! It was exhilarating. The wildness and power of nature was like nothing she had ever experienced. It had taken nearly six hours, but she had done it. Now she was walking on the highest point in the United Kingdom.

As they moved towards the mountain's peak and the ruined observatory, a patch of mist suddenly cleared and the mouth of a gully opened only metres away. Sara stopped. The wind grew even angrier. Her father walked on, hunched forward. She swayed, tugged and pulled by the furious gale.

For those who were lost, the gully's ragged jaws were waiting. One step too far, then nothing for 600 metres. She stared, mesmerised. Like a dream, the gully's edge crept closer. There lay death. There lay never-ending darkness. And yet she did not turn away. The nothingness, the emptiness was just a few steps in front of her. 'Come,' it beckoned, 'come closer.' The void was singing, a howl that reached into her stomach. Sara could *feel* it. The gully's dark innards were calling, begging her to step just a little closer, move just a little off the path. She shook her head. Took a step back. But then another voice was there. Beside her. In her ear. The boy's. A whisper, but clear and strong.

'Shaaann Wuuuu.'

Once again, like a fragment of iron standing before a huge magnet, she could feel her whole body being drawn forward. But this wasn't a photograph of Chan before her – it was the edge of a cliff and every molecule in her was straining, pulling, tugging her towards it.

She staggered forward. 'No! No!' she cried, helpless to prevent it.

'Shaaaan Wuuuuu.' The voice filled her head, drowning the roar of the wind.

She felt her legs move again. Another step. She stared down into the gully, a centimetre from the precipice. Mist-like smoke raced up towards her, shrouding her. Her heels rocked. Below her right foot, a rock squirmed out, toppled over the edge and, falling into air, it disappeared silently, as though it had never existed.

'Shaaan Wuuuuu.' The sound vibrated in her head.

*Make it stop! Make it stop!* The scream in her throat would not come. Another rock, below her left foot, fell away, lost in an instant.

'Sara! Sara!' High above the howling wind, her father's voice called to her. Sara turned. Her father grabbed her wrist. Heaving her from the edge and gaining momentum even though the wind was against them, he dragged her away from gully. 'What were you doing?' he shouted, holding on tightly to both her arms. 'What were you doing?' He was furious, Sara could see that.

Momentarily, she was too shaken to focus on his face. Somehow she managed to mumble, 'I'm sorry.' But then a rising tide of anger brought her back to her senses. He had tried to kill her. This boy, this...thing had reached out, thousands of miles away from her home in Beijing, and almost succeeded in forcing her off a cliff. If she wasn't safe in Scotland, where was she safe? The thought of a dark force acting against her was chilling, truly terrifying, in fact. But...so what if she was scared? She wasn't afraid to admit it. And so what if this thing had powers she had never imagined?

If it wanted a war, it was going to get one!

# CHAPTER 46

—

'It'll be tougher climbing down,' her father said just before they left the summit.

Sara gawped at him. It had taken them nearly four hours of hard climbing to get to the top. Her legs, so exhausted they were trembling, were telling her that they wanted to surrender, that she should sit down and rest and not consider getting up for at least a couple of days.

Her father shrugged. 'Just being realistic,' he said. 'You're usually tired after climbing to the top, and you'll be using a slightly different muscle set to go down. The ground being slippery after all the rain doesn't help either.' He gave an apologetic shrug.

Sara said nothing. *How could going down possibly be as difficult as going up?* she thought.

But annoyingly, her father was absolutely right. A few hundred metres of descent told her that. It was really, really hard – much harder than she expected. Muscles were aching that she didn't know she had, and she was unbelievably tired – physically tired, but mentally, too.

Since the cliff face, her brain had replayed the incident over and over. One step more and she would have been dead. Her father would never have forgiven himself. It would have destroyed her mother, too. *Who was Shan Wu? Was that the creep's name?* Until she found out otherwise, she would assume it was. How exactly she was going to deal with him, she'd worry about later. First, she needed to get off the mountain safely. But controlling her descent and making sure she placed her feet carefully and didn't stumble and fall – which might have meant a broken wrist or worse – took a huge amount of concentration and energy, both of which were in very, *very* short supply. If that weren't bad enough, she also had a blister on her big toe. It had started almost as soon as the descent began. And now, each time she slowed down or turned direction or stepped awkwardly, she could feel it – a sharp stab of pain that rose all the way up her leg. Had she been on a street, or in a mall, she would have stopped and refused to go any further. But up here, on the mountain, after more than six hours of ascending and descending, after the punishment her body had endured, the blister was just that: a blister. She was determined it wouldn't stop her, or even slow her down – and she definitely wasn't going to whine about it. Instead, she told herself to focus on what was in front of her. 'Focus,' she told herself, 'and take everything one step at a time.'

After following her father off the summit and past the scree, Sara put down her hood. The rain had eased. It hadn't stopped completely – there was still a smirr, as her father called it – but it was much lighter than before. In front of them was Halfway Lochan. It had taken them about an hour and a half to get there, and there was still more than an hour's descent to complete. 'Just our luck,' her father said, looking up at the lighter sky. 'Pity it didn't clear while we were up there.'

Sara nodded, deep in thought. Before, it seemed that every time she saw a picture of Chan, she was transported to where Shan Wu was. Why was that? When she was in the scroll, the Immortals had said stuff about fighting Chan and his confederates. Was Shan Wu a confederate of Chan's? And what about when she was at the top of the Ben? How had Shan Wu been able to get inside her head? Was she still in danger? Her family? How great were his powers? Did he have to wait until she was in a dangerous situation before he could attack her? If so, climbing another mountain would be a *bad* idea! It made her clench her jaw in frustration, but right now all these questions were unanswerable. She had to do *something*. But what? In the end, there was only one thing she could do: spend some serious time researching Chan that night.

Feeling a bit better because she had a plan, she stared up at the sky. The weather definitely was brightening. Was she disappointed that she hadn't seen the view from the top? Well, a little. The panorama would have been amazing. But on the other hand, experiencing that weather – its power, its changeability – had also been amazing, and it had given her the feeling that she had succeeded not only against the wishes of the mountain but the weather too…

By the time they reached the car, the sun was throwing brilliant, geometric shafts of light onto the rolling hills. As they sat half-in, half-out of the car, untying their boots, her father's phone rang.

'Your mother,' he said before answering. Sara listened as her father spoke. 'Yup… Yup… Did she make it?' her father said, repeating her mother's question and smiling at Sara.

Sara smiled back.

'She sure did,' her father answered. 'She sure did.'

That evening after dinner, Sara left her parents and went into the garden of Loch Linnhe House. A well-kept lawn stretched the length of the walled garden. At the end of the lawn, ferns and several small trees grew. In the branches of the trees, like tiny balls of fluff, sparrows bounced, chirping noisily and arguing about their perch for the night. By the house, next to where Sara stood, two wicker chairs faced one another. She shivered and wrapped her arms around herself. Even though the sun was more than an hour away from setting, the air was cool and still.

She chose the chair that faced east and gave a view of the Ben. Stiffly, she sat down. The Ben was transformed. Now it was a sullen monster, darker and more menacing than at any time during the day. Sara could hardly believe she had been to the top of it and back down. It didn't seem possible that someone could climb such a beast, least of all someone who had never climbed a mountain in her life before. She felt tired but good; nothing she had ever done had been as physically challenging as climbing the Ben. She didn't think she would become a regular hill-walker – perhaps one mountain was enough. But that was fine. She couldn't wait to show Lily the pictures she had taken.

She was reaching for her mobile to check the photos and video from climbing the Ben when she heard Mrs Morton enter the kitchen behind her. Through the kitchen's open window, Sara could hear Mrs Morton humming a tune. Water ran. Turning, Sara saw Mrs Morton filling a kettle under the tap. Unaware that Sara was watching, Mrs Morton switched on the kettle, picked up a remote and switched on the small TV hanging in a corner of the kitchen. Soundlessly, it burst into life. A man in a suit was talking behind a desk. Below him, a banner was reporting share prices. A business news programme. *Boring,* thought Sara. She was about to turn back and face the garden when she stopped. It was a report about Bai Lu. Suddenly, in her mind she was in the same dark, claustrophobic space. Once again, she searched the darkness, heart pounding, knowing something was there with her, unseen yet deeply menacing…

From out of the darkness, she heard laughter, a high-pitched and manic chuckling.

'I know who you are!' she shouted.

The laugh dwindled and died.

'You are Shan Wu, aren't you?' Her heart was thumping so hard, it was making her words sound shaky.

'Shaaan Wuuuu,' came the reply, fetid air blowing across her face and ruffling her hair.

She stared into the darkness, but could see nothing. 'Where is this place? How did you get here?'

But almost as quickly as the vision came, it disappeared. Sara looked at the TV; the report had ended.

Something rustled behind her. She swivelled round, fists bunched... and sighed. A small grey rabbit had bounced out of the ferns and onto the lawn and was now nibbling daintily at the grass, its long ears sticking straight up. Sara smiled. Suddenly, as though a magician had tipped them out of a top hat, two more rabbits joined the first. As Sara watched, the three rabbits hopped and bounced until they were gathered in a loose semi-circle. Slowly the smile faded. The three rabbits had raised their heads and trained their dark, glittering eyes on her. They were staring – unblinking, unmoving – at Sara, their eyes locked on hers.

Sara swallowed. 'Unbelievable,' she whispered, raising her mobile as smoothly as she could, but before she could press the record button the rabbits dispersed, scattering randomly across the lawn. Heads down, they nibbled at the grass. Sara lowered her mobile. As soon as she did, the three rabbits reformed, gathering in a semi-circle, their small eyes staring at her. This was too weird. This was—

'Sara!'

Sara jumped.

'Mrs Morton's wondering what you'd like for breakfast tomorrow,' Sara's mother said, standing at the kitchen doorway.

'Did you see that? Did you see what they did?' Sara said, eyes wide, pointing over her shoulder.

'See what?' her mother asked.

Sara turned back. Her jaw dropped.

The three rabbits had disappeared.

Sara looked at her mother, who was smiling at her. 'It doesn't matter.'

'Are you alright? You look a little pale,' her mother asked.

Sara gave a feeble smile. Strange things were happening. They might all be in danger. But she knew her mum would be there if she needed her. Knowing that gave her strength. And what had she done to show her appreciation? She'd wedged a lie between them. *You know what?* she thought to herself, *I'm sick of this!* She took a deep breath. 'Mum?'

'Yes, dear.'

'You know how I said I was sick – just before school finished?'

'Mmmm.' Her mother gave her a quizzical look.

Sara swallowed. 'Well, I wasn't. The truth is I wanted to go to the Lufthansa mall with Annette and her dad and the rest of the girls for pizza. So I pretended to be ill. When you left for work, I sneaked out and sneaked back in again before you and dad got home.' Sara looked at her mum. 'I'm sorry. I should have gone to Granny Tang's. I shouldn't have lied.'

'Oh,' Sara's mum said and stared at Sara. 'Well, I can't pretend I'm not angry with you. But at least you've finally told me the truth. So why *did* you lie?' she asked.

Sara shrugged. 'I thought it was boring – visiting Granny Tang, I mean.'

'You thought, or you think?'

'I thought. I don't think that any more.'

Sara's mother tucked her reading glasses into her hair and looked at Sara. When she spoke, her voice was calm. 'You're not a child any more, Sara. It *is* time you took more responsibility, and that means being allowed to make more decisions for yourself. So… what I'm saying is *you* have to decide whether you want to go to Granny Tang's or not – I won't make you go there if you don't want to.'

'Mum, I do,' she said. 'I really do.'

# CHAPTER 47

From her bedroom window, Sara gazed out across Loch Linnhe House's back garden to the distant Ben. Although the sun had set and it was after ten o'clock, the sky was still quite bright in the west, its luminescent blue just a few shades darker than it had been during the day. To the east, however, the sky, and the Ben, were shadow-filled already.

Midges – small, swarming flies with disproportionately large teeth – were drifting through the window, seeking the flesh around her ears and forehead and sucking her blood. Closing the window, she rubbed where they had bitten. In the next bedroom, she heard her parents' muffled voices and the noise of their window being closed too. She was glad she had told her mother about Pizzapie, glad to get it off her conscience. As soon as she got back to Beijing, she would go and visit Granny Tang. Apart from the promise she had made to her mother, she really wanted to ask Granny Tang more about the Immortals. She snorted. Imagine telling Granny Tang she had met Zhang Guolao and He Xiangu. Good idea – NOT!

She shivered. The warm duvet beckoned. Instead of getting into bed, she opened the browser on her mobile and, careful not to choose articles with pictures, began to search for more information about Chan. When she had researched him the first time back in Beijing, she had merely been curious. But things were different now. First, the Immortals had mentioned Chan's name. Second, Shan Wu had tried to force her to step off the cliff on the

Ben, and that made her angry. What was the connection between Chan and Shan Wu? Was Shan Wu one of Chan's confederates? The Immortals hadn't told her. It didn't matter. She was going to find out. And then? She'd figure that out later. Right now, there was only one thing to do.

She had to find out more about Chan and his company, Bai Lu.

Slowly, Sara put her phone down on top of her bed. She folded her arms and crossed her legs. Her foot swung, flicking up and down like an angry cat's tail. She had found out loads.

Bai Lu was based in Dunhuang, not far away from the world-famous Mogao Caves in China. The company was spending millions of dollars researching gene therapy treatments and three of Bai Lu's executives had been arrested for conducting clinical trials in which experimental and unlicensed treatments had been given to 42 volunteers, of whom nine had later died. What was the purpose of the trials? What kind of gene therapy were they testing? That had remained secret. Chan had denied all knowledge of the research program. The executives, who had recently pled guilty, also denied that Chan knew anything about what they were doing, which struck Sara as convenient for Chan. Chillingly, the three Bai Lu executives, held in separate prisons, had been found dead in their cells *all on the same morning*. That had happened only a few days ago. Nevertheless, the official verdict had been suicide.

As for why Chan was in El Salvador mining fingerite, there was less information. However, she did find out that fingerite was once considered an essential ingredient in the medicines created by the people around the Izalco volcano. And what had they used it for? That question had taken longer to answer. Local legend said the brownish-red mineral from the fumaroles, or openings, around the mouth of the volcano promised long life...

The final article she had read was the most interesting. According to it, Chan could trace his lineage back to two brothers from the Song Dynasty – a fact that he often boasted about. The article said he enjoyed naming the two brothers who were his ancestors. It was when Sara read the names that she jumped off the bed in excitement. One was called Shan Tuo. And the other? Shan Wu – the terrifying boy she had seen floating towards her.

Of course, when she had thought about it more, she calmed down. There were lots of people with that name – in fact, there were probably thousands alive right now. And how many were there in all of history? Millions! If the floating boy was one of Chan's relatives, why didn't he have the same genetic condition that Chan had? The floating boy's face had been horrible, but it had been the face of a boy about the same age as her; definitely not a prematurely old one like Chan's. So not every member of a family gets afflicted by a genetic disease. What had that TED talk she'd watched recently in class said about recessive genes? *Think!* Something like: if the trait was recessive, it meant there was a one in four chance that the members of the next generation would show the symptoms of the condition. So… Shan Wu could be an ancestor of Chan's, but not one who showed symptoms of the condition. Which meant… Shan Wu might or might not be related to Chan? She pursed her lips in frustration. *This is getting me nowhere*, she thought. Then another thought struck her: the genetic condition might have entered Chan's family much later through one of Chan's more recent ancestors, which meant that even if Shan Wu were related to Chan, there was no reason why he would be prematurely aged.

She sighed. Trying to prove a connection this way was a waste of time, and her brain was beginning to hurt with all the thinking! But there was something about the image of the floating boy that was nagging her. It had hooked her brain and was refusing to let go.

What was it? She felt like one part of her mind was showing her the answer to a question the other part didn't know about. What was she not seeing?

Once again, she recalled the dark holes where the boy's eyes should have been, the tongue that flicked and probed like a serpent, his grotesquely long nails, the hand reaching out towards her…

THE HAND REACHING OUT TOWARDS HER!

She slapped her forehead and grabbed her mobile phone. Furiously, she searched through its browsing history. It was so obvious! A moment later, she found what she was looking for: a picture of the Bai Lu headquarters. With her right thumb and index finger, she enlarged the picture. And there it was in Chinese characters, the corporate motto of Bai Lu emblazoned across the top of the building: *Establish the hegemon*.

Exactly the same characters she had seen on the floating boy's arm when she had been on the bus.

She nodded, smiled, clapped her hands together. It could mean only one thing: Shan Wu, the floating boy, *was* Chan's ancestor.

'Of course he is!' Sara whispered to herself. But what did *that* mean? Was she expected to fight *both* of them? She rubbed her eyes. Outside, it was properly dark, with leaden clouds obscuring the stars and threatening rain. She yawned. How she had managed to stay awake this late after climbing the Ben she had no idea. Adrenaline? She glanced at her leg. It was still crossed and still bobbing up and down. Yup, definitely adrenaline – but because something else was bugging her! She groaned. She knew she wouldn't be able to get to sleep unless she figured out what it was.

She forced her mind to start from the beginning. What did she know about Shan Wu and Shan Tuo? The answer was very little. In Google Scholar, she typed in *Song Dynasty + Shan Wu*. A quick scan of the results yielded nothing particularly interesting. She tried again, this time with *Song Dynasty + Shan Tuo*. Her heart sank a little when she saw 27 pages of results. Taking a deep breath, she began scrolling through them. She was on page 12 when a paper in an obscure academic journal called *Ancient Chinese Manuscripts and Scrolls* caught her eye. The paper's title was *The Jinshi – Chinese Civil Service Exams*. She downloaded the PDF and started reading. It had been written by a professor from Shanghai University. According to him, during the Song Dynasty, thousands of people took the twice-yearly civil service exam. If the examinee passed, he was allowed to become an official and join the government. However, the exam, on philosophy and classical literature, was really tough and only the best students succeeded. Her eyes roamed over the document until they found the name Shan Tuo. It was in an extract from a diary written by a wealthy, influential woman around 1009 CE.

Breathlessly, Sara read what had been written more than a thousand years ago.

*Advanced scholar Shan Tuo, who was awarded the title Zhuangyuan when he achieved the highest grade in all China and admitted to the Imperial Palace bureaucracy, the most esteemed in the land, has fallen from grace. Poor Shan Tuo! How I wish it were not true. So clever but so greedy! Corruption is an evil that must be eradicated. I must approve of Shan Tuo's dismissal. And yet with his old man's face and young body, I still pity him. Some say he has gone to his home village. Perhaps the shame will kill him. Others say he prospers, having formed the vicious, law-breaking Gang of the White Fawn.*

Sara closed the PDF and shook her head slowly, incredulous at her failure to see the significance of Chan's company name sooner. Now, of course, it was as plain as the nose on her face: in English, Bai Lu meant 'white deer'. And a fawn – as in Gang of the White Fawn – was the term for a young deer!

Against her will, she yawned again. Although her body was aching and the muscles in her legs were already telling her she was going to have a hard time walking tomorrow, she felt good. She was certain that the floating boy, Shan Wu, was Chan's ancestor. She had also discovered that Chan's genetic condition came from Shan Wu's brother, Shan Tuo. And she knew that Chan's business empire was called Bai Lu for a reason: money from Shan Tuo's criminal gang had started the family business all those years ago! Amazing!

She noticed her foot was no longer jiggling. Thank goodness!

She looked at her bed. Time to get some sleep. She deserved it! Smiling while she crawled into it, she pulled the duvet over her head and closed her eyes, enjoying the pillow's soft coolness against her cheek.

Far away, an oystercatcher cried. His rapid, lonely calls echoed across the silent landscape.

Moments later, still wondering what part she was supposed to play in all of this, Sara was fast asleep.

# PART 7

# BEIJING, CHINA
## THE PRESENT DAY

# CHAPTER 48

—

Sara leaned forward, peering down as the wings of the jet slowly returned to the horizontal, revealing the Thames – a blue-grey ribbon – passing several thousand metres below her. There was the London Eye, the Houses of Parliament, Battersea Power Station, the Tate Modern, and the docklands growing ever smaller as the jet gained altitude. So that was it. The summer holidays were over. It was twenty past seven in the evening. They were due to arrive in Beijing just after midday. Unbelievable. Where had the summer gone?

Not that it had been uneventful. Far from it! She'd climbed the highest mountain in Britain, almost been killed, discovered more about Shan Wu, met some Immortals, acquired a silk dagger and a silvery slice, researched a man called Chan whose company was established by Shan Tuo, the brother of Shan Wu… She had also seen Martin Fröst in concert at the Wigmore Hall and visited all the London sights with Granny Livingstone. Not bad for five weeks!

Beside her, her dad folded his arms. His eyelids were already drooping. Trust him! On his right, Sara's mother had her cabin light on, its beam illuminating the book she was engrossed in. The jet climbed higher. The fasten-seat-belts sign was turned off and the cabin crew began preparing the food in the kitchen.

Sara unbuckled her seatbelt and sighed. She felt a bit torn. Although she had really enjoyed the holiday and would gladly have stayed longer, she was also looking forward to seeing Lily again, and Joaquin. She wondered what he had discovered about fingerite and

Chan's reasons for mining it. One thing was for sure: they would have loads to talk about. She hadn't learned anything about turtles, or the differences between zooplankton and phytoplankton for that matter, but now she could at least discuss Bai Lu. Glancing up, she thought about the silk dagger and the silvery slice, both of which were above her head in the luggage rack, safely tucked away in her small case. On the outward journey, airport security hadn't asked her about the slice – and probably thought it was just jewellery. The inward journey was the same: security at Heathrow hadn't asked her about it either. Phew!

Several more times during the holidays she had tried to turn the piece of silk into a dagger. She hadn't really expected it to work – and it hadn't. Not that she particularly wanted to have a deadly weapon in her hands. Even the thought of the silk blade's lethal sharpness made her shudder. Still, she had wanted to see if she could do it, and her failure was almost as annoying as the vague answers she had received from Zhang Guolao and He Xiangu. What had He Xiangu said? Something about needing to find the other two hares? How *exactly* was she supposed to do that?

That evening, after arriving in Beijing, having a snooze, a shower, something to eat, and checking the school website, Sara went to see her grandmother. Looking through the double-glazed windows in Granny Tang's apartment, Sara watched as the sun sank slowly over the city. The view over Beijing was beautiful. The sun, huge and golden, bathed the city in its soft, yellow light. High above in the blushing sky, an airliner glinted for a moment, a tiny speck in the heavens. Sara watched it as it slowly faded to invisibility.

'Sara?'

Sara turned and watched as Granny Tang crossed the room carrying a flickering taper towards a small table on which their ancestral tablet sat, as red and gold as the sun and sky outside. The tablet was surrounded by old black and white photographs, a small painting of a valley, and half a dozen incense sticks. Her grandmother began murmuring a report of what had happened recently in her life to the photograph of her dead husband, Sara's grandfather, while she lit the first incense stick.

Sara listened with half an ear to her grandmother's words, watching as one after the other, the incense sticks sent smoke spiralling into the air. Sandalwood, star anise, cedar – the scents reminded her of the incense that burned in the graveyard when she met the monk, the surprise she felt when the Immortals revealed themselves. As she stood and breathed in the fragrant air, her thoughts wandered back to the look of delight on her grandmother's face when she had opened the door and found Sara on the doorstep. It made her realise how few times she had visited her unannounced and voluntarily.

'Shall we sit down?' asked her grandmother, finishing her prayers and pointing to the sofa.

Sara smiled and followed her grandmother. On a table next to the sofa was a black and red lacquer tray with a pot of tea and two bowls on it. Granny Tang poured and Sara smelled the sweet jasmine.

Settling into the sofa, Granny Tang raised the bowl to her lips and blew on the hot tea just as there was a loud thump, and a painting that had been hanging on the wall behind them fell to the floor.

Granny Tang barely blinked. She took a noisy sip of the jasmine tea. 'Ghosts,' she said, shrugging. 'Things happen.'

'Ghosts…' Sara whispered, remembering He Xiangu's words: 'You can call us spirits.' She stared at her grandmother. Still muttering, she continued sipping her tea intermittently, oblivious to Sara's all-consuming desire to know *everything* about the Eight Immortals.

Granny Tang threw a glance at her granddaughter. 'You alright?' she asked. 'You look funny.'

'Fine, absolutely fine! Who are the Immortals?' Sara asked.

'The Immortals?' repeated Granny Tang. 'Are you telling me you don't know who the Immortals are?' She gave her small head three or four rapid shakes. 'What *are* they teaching you at that school?' she said, banging down her bowl. She gave Sara a withering look before continuing. 'The Eight Immortals were a group of legendary beings who bestowed life and defeated evil. Do you know *that*?'

Sara shrugged. 'I don't know as much as I should.'

Granny Tang tutted. 'He Xiangu, Cao Guojiu, Li Tieguai, Lan Caihe, Lu Dongbin, Han Xiang Zi, Zhang Guolao, and Zhongli Quan. You should remember these names!'

Smiling, Sara watched as Granny Tang settled back in her chair.

The lecture was about to begin.

Sara couldn't have felt happier.


The more Granny Tang told Sara about the Eight Immortals, the more interested she became. How had she not asked more about Chinese legendary beings before? The tales about them were fantastic: He Xiangu, who ate mica and carried a lotus flower; Han Xiang Zi, who loved the Chinese flute; Li Tieguai, who was old with a scraggly beard and who cured the sick with a gourd; Zhang Guolao, who liked to snatch birds in flight and make himself invisible... And the others too. Sara had enjoyed listening to tales about them all.

Nevertheless, her mind hadn't been solely on the tales, not a hundred per cent of the time. As though a lasso had been tied around her brain, her thoughts throughout the visit had been pulled back to the two objects hidden in the desk in her bedroom. What was she supposed to do with those? They made her feel anxious every time she looked at them, and she looked at them often! There was the other thing, too – should she tell Lily about what happened in the scroll, or not?

Finally, Granny Tang finished her stories, stood up, and with her usual bluntness announced it was time for Sara to leave. Sara smiled and kissed her grandmother goodbye. Outside the apartment, with her grandmother's door closing behind her, she strode across the hall and pressed the button on the lift, watching the floor numbers light up as they heralded the lift's ascent.

*BING!* The lift arrived and its doors opened. She smiled, feeling content. It had taken her a bit of time, but she had finally made up her mind. She would do the thing she had been thinking about doing! Dealing with all of this was too much for her. She needed advice. She needed help from someone whom she knew could keep a secret. She would tell Lily – show her the piece of silk and the silvery slice, let her into the secret she had been carrying by herself for five long weeks, hear what she had to say.

It was the right decision.


That night, after preparing her clothes and her school bag for the first day of the new term, she sat down at her computer and typed in *Three Hares + China*. She hit enter and stared, open mouthed, at the screen.

'Wow!'

There were hundreds of thousands of hits about the Three Hares and the Silk Road. Clicking on one of the links, she read hungrily. The Silk Road was a 4,000-mile trade route that had grown because the West wanted silk and spices, and for a long time, only China knew how to make silk. That she knew already. She clicked another link. It talked about a symbol, the triskelion, which could be found all along the Silk Road – in Russia, Iran, Germany and England to name a few – and which may have originated in ancient China. According to the Wikipedia page, it represented peace and tranquillity. She clicked another link, jumped to a Wikipedia entry for the Three Hares and scrolled down the page.

She gasped. There was a symbol composed of three interlocking hares: each leaping forward, their ears pointing up, their legs running. She leaned back. Her head was like a beehive as thoughts buzzed between her ears. The slice she had been given showed one of these hares… She rubbed her tired eyes. There were so many questions she wanted answered, and one of the biggest of them all was what she was supposed to do next. She had been asked to contact two more Hares. How? How would she ever find them?

She reached in her drawer and pulled out the slice. For some reason, her computer was making that buzzing noise again. Argh! How annoying! She gave the monitor a slap. It did no good. Giving up, she switched on the reading lamp next to her and directed its brilliant beam onto the silvery slice, but no matter how hard she searched it, no matter how slowly she forced her eyes to crawl over its surface, the slice offered her no clues. She did the same with the piece of silk. The result was the same. Realising that she had to get up early and knowing she was no nearer to answering any of the questions flying around her head, she put both the objects back in the drawer, switched off the computer, and crawled into bed.

Her alarm was set for 6am.

Head on the pillow, she closed her eyes and listened. There were no distant oystercatchers calling, only the hum of the air-conditioning unit and whisper of the ceiling fan's blades gently parting the air…

At least her computer wasn't buzzing as loudly.

# Chapter 49

—

The first day of the new term began with the bus turning up late. Great start! When it did finally arrive, its doors slammed open and Sara hopped on, glad to get out of the humidity. But the good mood she was in and the smile she was wearing quickly slid away when she looked up and down the bus. There was no sign of Lily or Joaquin anywhere. Where were they?

Choosing a seat near the driver – as far away as possible from the Ferdinand brothers, who of course *were* there – she immediately texted Lily. According to Lily's speedy reply, her father was giving her a lift to school this morning. She'd see Sara in the first lesson.

*OK, c u then,* Sara typed, followed by some smiley faces.

A second later, her phone pinged as Lily replied. *Lookn 4wrd 2 seeing u.*

*U 2,* Sara answered and rested the phone on her lap. Gazing out of the front of the bus, she wondered if Joaquin's father was taking him to school, too. She had tried texting him the night before, asking if he was ready for the new term, but hadn't received a reply. Not that it surprised her – Joaquin was a self-confessed 'rubbish correspondent'. She'd ask him all about his holidays when she saw him. Once again, she thought about how useless and embarrassed she had felt before the summer holidays when Lily and Joaquin had discussed Chan. That time, she had been totally unable to add anything to the conversation. Well, things had changed. There was loads that she had discovered and couldn't wait to share.

Today, she had a simple plan: not fall asleep in any of her classes – because of the jet lag she was feeling; not let her stomach rumble; ask Lily to come back to her apartment; show Lily the things the Immortals had given her, and—

A tap on the shoulder interrupted her thoughts. She turned. The Gerbil's dark little eyes stared into hers. Next to her, Jaz was watching her too, an expectant glint in her eyes.

'What?' Sara asked, annoyed. She didn't like talking to The Gerbil at the best of times and she especially didn't want to talk to her now, not when she had so many other things to think about.

'Heard about your boyfriend. Too bad,' The Gerbil said, making the fakest of fake sad faces.

'What are you talking about?'

The Gerbil and Jaz, eyebrows raised, exchanged amused glances. 'Your boyfriend,' The Gerbil said slyly. 'We heard he's not coming back.'

'What boyfriend? I don't have a boyfriend,' Sara snapped, only just managing not to add 'you idiot'.

The Gerbil's grin widened. 'Oh, didn't you know? Joaquin's father has been reposted. They're all off to sunny *España. Olé! Ándale! Ándale!* she cried, raising her hands as though she were holding imaginary castanets – or was it a red rag to a bull? Jaz punched The Gerbil on the arm and, as Sara watched in disgust, they dissolved into gales of screeching laughter.

'Why would I believe *anything* you say?' Sara said icily when The Gerbil and Jaz paused to breathe.

Wiping her eyes, The Gerbil slowly leaned forward. ''Cause my mother and Joaquin's mother used to be in the same yoga class, and just after the summer holidays started she told my mother that Joaquin's father's been posted to Spain and that they've already found a new school for Joaquin in Madrid. *That's* why!'

Sara spun around in her seat. Trying her best to ignore the sniggers and snorts coming from behind her, and trying not to let them see she was texting, she sent Lily a message. *Is J still in Bjing?*

A second later, she had Lily's response. *Think so. Y?*

*Gerbil sayn in Spain.*

*Nah! She's full of…seeds :)*

But Sara wasn't so sure. *Not heard from him.*

*Me neither.*

*Does The G's mum know J's?*

*Yeah, think so – go yoga 2gether.*

When Sara read that, she dropped her phone onto her lap. The yoga thing didn't mean The Gerbil was telling the truth, but… perhaps Joaquin really *had* gone.

'Checked out my info with your buddy Lily yet?' It was The Gerbil.

'Why don't you just shut up?'

The Gerbil snorted. 'Loser,' she said and slowly leaned back.

For the rest of the journey, Sara sat silently watching the road as the bus chewed through the traffic and swallowed the miles.

# CHAPTER 50

—

'So he really has gone to Spain without even saying goodbye?'

Sara and Lily were in the corridor walking away from their fourth class of the morning. There was a break of thirty minutes before the next one. The time out couldn't have come sooner for Sara. The jet lag was really hitting hard and she was feeling about as energetic as a sponge – cake, marine animal, or washing implement, take your pick. Around her, there was the usual riot of noise with everyone desperate to welcome their friends back and catch up with the all the gossip. She needed to grab a quick coffee from the vending machine if she was to have any chance of staying awake. She glanced at her watch. She'd have to hurry.

'Looks like it,' Lily said, pursing her lips. Then added, 'I'm sorry. I guess you really liked him.'

Sara didn't know what to say. She shrugged.

Lily continued. 'I could ask The Gerbil for his mother's number if—'

'No,' Sara interrupted. 'Don't do that. If he wants to contact me, he knows my number and email address.'

'Okay. Sure.'

They walked on in silence for a while.

'So did you have a good holiday?' Lily asked.

Sara smiled and nodded. 'You?'

'Oh yeah!' Lily cried. 'It was *amazing*! You should have seen—'

'I'm glad,' Sara interrupted, embarrassed. 'Sorry, it's just... I don't have much time and…' She lowered her eyes. '… I've got a favour to ask.'

'Sure! Fire away!' Lily cried.

'Can you come back to my place after school? There's something I need to show you.'

Lily's smile wavered. Her eyes flicked onto Sara's face. Sara knew the tone of her request had alerted her friend.

'I can't really explain here. I need to show you.'

'That sounds a bit… ominous,' Lily said. 'Are you okay?'

In her mind, Sara saw the lethally sharp dagger that He Xiangu had created when she shook the piece of silk. 'Maybe. I don't know. I really don't know.'

'You're worrying me,' Lily said, taking hold of Sara's arm. 'What is it?'

'Just come back with me. Will you?'

'Of course I will!'

'Thanks,' Sara said. 'I really appreciate it.' She glanced at her watch again. 'Look, I've got to meet someone…'

'Oooooh,' Lily said, her eyebrows raised and a tell-me-more look on her face.

Sara scuttled away, calling over her shoulder, 'I'll meet you outside A6, okay?' She didn't hear Lily's reply.

Sara sat the cup of coffee from the vending machine on the flat, wooden arm of the lecture chair and took a deep breath, trying to relax as she waited for the first question. Her hand had shaken and some coffee had spilled. She looked around. Just her luck – a classroom without tissues. Using the side of her hand, she flicked away the droplets. She had just disposed of the last one when the classroom door flew open and someone she didn't recognise stuck his head in, glanced around, and disappeared again, slamming the door shut behind him. She glanced at Joshua. He didn't seem to notice. She looked at her watch. There were ten minutes remaining of the thirty-minute break and the muted noises outside the classroom – the chattering, the laughing, the screeching – were slowly diminishing as the start of the next class approached. Inside the classroom, the loudest noises that Sara could hear were the sound of her own heart thudding in her ears and the occasional sniff from Joshua, head down, shuffling through several stacks of papers spread across the desk in front of him. She balanced her fingertips on the lip of the plastic cup – because she was terrified she would forget about it, move, and overturn it – and continued to wait.

Joshua, the editor of *Today!*, flicked hair away from his eyes and tutted. Was he trying to find her application? Trying to find a set of questions he wanted to ask? What was he looking for? She poured some sugar into the coffee and stirred it with a little wooden stick. The cup was almost too hot to hold and the brown liquid in it was barely fit for human consumption, but if nothing else, it offered her a psychological boost: the caffeine would increase her alertness and sharpen her thinking, or so she thought. 'I need all the help I can get,' she muttered. She glanced at her mobile and realised she hadn't had a look at *Word of the Day*. She opened the app and immediately wished she hadn't.

*Debacle – an inglorious failure.*

'Ah ha!' Joshua cried, pulled a document out of the pile, and began studying it intently.

Sara closed her mobile. The advert for the job had been on the school noticeboard and website since before the summer holidays. Seeing it was still on the site before she visited Granny Tang the night before, Sara had surprised herself by sending a brief CV and cover letter to Joshua. It had seemed like a great idea at the time.

But now, sitting waiting for the interview with him to begin, she was wondering why she had done it. Why *had* she done it?

'So…' Joshua said.

Sara jumped; his voice was surprisingly loud and assured.

'…you'd like to join *Today!*

Sara nodded. 'Yes, I feel—' *Listen to my voice! It's trembling!* '—I feel I could be invaluable.' *OMG! Invaluable! INVALUABLE!* 'I mean, useful, because…'

Joshua, smiling, flicked his hair and leaned forward, both elbows on the desk. 'Because?'

'Because… because I love English – and because I recently investigated a company that—'

'Oh?' Joshua put his head down and scribbled something.

'Yeah. It was, I mean, it *is* a multinational that recently began operating in El Salvador near the Izalco volcano. And—'

Joshua looked up again.

'—and this is a problem because the facility there was built near protected beaches, so it's had an impact on wildlife such as the leatherback turtle.' Sara took a breath.

'Is it a local company?'

'It's based in Dunhuang.'

Joshua scribbled some more. He looked up again and nodded. 'Interesting. So, you're interested in environmentalism?'

'Well, no. I mean, yes. Indirectly. But I'm more interested in the owner of the company, Chan. Recently, three of the company's executives, who were jailed pending trial, were found dead in their prison cells. They were all being held in separate prisons, yet they all died on the same day. According to the prison authorities, they committed suicide.'

Joshua raised an eyebrow.

Sara continued. 'The executives were charged with conducting illegal experiments, using volunteers who hadn't been properly briefed

– they were basically guinea pigs. Nine of them died later. When I researched the origins of Chan's company, I found out that—'

Joshua held up a hand. Sara stopped.

'Look,' Joshua said, putting down his pen and rubbing his chin, 'to be honest, you might be a little over-qualified for the job. We're after a deputy editor, but, well, we aren't the *Washington Post* and there isn't anyone working on *Today!* called Bernstein or Woodward.'

Sara frowned. *Who were Bernstein and Woodward?*

'What I'm saying,' Joshua continued, 'is we don't really *do* investigative journalism. It's more like book and film reviews, articles about teachers, articles about courses, local events – that sort of thing.' His voice trailed off.

Sara could feel her chances slipping away. No! She wasn't going to allow that to happen. This wasn't going to be a debacle! She really, really wanted the job. She had gathered her courage and applied for it. She had done some good research on Chan. She had things to say and was planning to be a journalist…

PLANNING!

Her eyes widened. For the first time since she had met the Immortals, Zhang Guolao's words echoed in her head again: 'Under our training, you've had opportunities to make and execute plans.' What had changed? Before the holidays, she wouldn't have had the nerve to apply. Well, look at her now! Here she was making plans, going for it… Win or lose, she was *trying*.

Her mouth was dry. Joshua was waiting, staring at her expectantly. She raised the cup and… the barest of ripples crossed the surface of the liquid. Her hand wasn't shaking. Not even a little. She sipped the hot liquid and put the cup down. She sat up straight and met Joshua's gaze. 'I promise I am going to work really, really hard. I'm planning be a journalist, and I'd love the opportunity to work at *Today!* Just give me a chance. That's all I want. If you don't like my work, fire me.'

The bell for the fourth class rang. Joshua looked down, gathered together the papers on the desk, took a deep breath. Then, rising slowly to his feet, he looked her straight in the eye. He shrugged, then smiled.

'Welcome to *Today!*

# CHAPTER 51

—

As soon as Sara and Lily opened the door to Sara's apartment, they heard aggressive voices bellowing at one another about someone being someone else's child.

Straining to raise her voice above the noise coming from the TV set in the living room, Sara cried, 'Hello, Mrs Ching,' and waited.

A moment later, Mrs Ching's small head – grey hair gathered in a tight bun – emerged from the living room and peeked around the door. She adjusted her thick glasses. 'Oh! Sara! You're home. You hungry? You want me to make something? Hello, Lily.'

'Hi, Mrs Ching,' said Lily. 'Enjoying the show?'

'Yes! Such a complicated family!'

'We're just… er, going to have a chat in my bedroom,' Sara said.

'Okay. Your mum said she will be back at nine, and your dad said he is coming home before eight.'

Sara nodded.

A fresh roar of denials turned Mrs Ching's head.

'See you later, Mrs Ching,' Lily cried.

Mrs Ching gave a quick wave and disappeared back into the living room.

In Sara's bedroom, Lily perched on the edge of Sara's bed and looked up at her friend. 'So, what is it you want to show me?'

Sara opened her mouth, but before she could say anything Lily cried, 'A text from Joaquin declaring his undying love for you! Show me! Show me!'

*If only it were that simple,* thought Sara. 'Calm down. I haven't heard anything from Joaquin, okay? And even if I had, it doubt it would be that!'

Lily looked crestfallen. 'Oh, okay. So what is it?'

'You promise you won't freak out?'

Lily's grin returned. 'Oooooh! Depends…'

'Promise!'

Lily held up her hands, still grinning. 'Okay, okay. I promise.'

Sara sat down next to her. Lily pushed her glasses onto the bridge of her nose and waited for Sara to speak. Sara took a deep breath. She gave a nervous laugh. 'I don't know where to begin. It's all been so crazy.'

Lily watched her silently.

Sara continued. 'I suppose the first time I *really* thought something weird was happening was just before the summer holidays. You were there, and Joaquin too. He was talking about the factory that was causing pollution and endangering turtles and he showed us a picture. Remember?'

Lily nodded. She looked like she was engrossed, like she was hanging on to every word that Sara said. How long would that last?

Dismissing that doubt, Sara began retelling her story – everything that had happened: the floating boy, her time in ancient China, her meeting with the Immortals, the fact that Shan Wu had tried to kill her on Ben Nevis – everything. As she spoke, she watched Lily's face carefully. With each new detail that Sara added, Lily's face began to change. Wide-eyed and astounded to begin with, Lily's look of amazement began to melt away and was slowly replaced by a wrinkling brow and narrowing, increasingly sceptical eyes. Worse was to follow. That look of puzzlement and suspicion slid away too and was replaced, to Sara's utter dismay, by something much, much worse: an ill-suppressed smirk. With her tightly pressed lips and downturned mouth, it was clear Lily was finding it very difficult indeed not to laugh. The more Sara talked about Immortals and hares and floating boys, the funnier Lily seemed to find it.

As soon as Sara finished, she shot to her feet. A flush of anger had reddened her face and quickened her pulse. It might all sound ridiculous but it was NO LAUGHING MATTER. She glared down at Lily, who, looking embarrassed, turned away and coughed. The two of them said nothing for a moment, the near silence broken only by the muted shouts and hoots coming from the TV in the living room.

Lily, turning to face Sara and making a very obvious and determined attempt to look serious, cleared her throat. 'It's… er… It's not…'

Sara held up a finger, silencing her. 'Wait!' she said, and spinning around she pulled open her computer desk's drawer. 'Just wait.' She dug around for a second until she found what she was looking for. Grabbing the silvery slice in her left hand and the piece of silk in her right, she turned and faced Lily. 'Look at these. He Xiangu and Zhang Guolao gave me them. Now do you believe me?' Not waiting for an answer, she stood in front of Lily and waited until Lily had slowly extended both her hands. When Lily's hands were open, Sara dropped both the items into them. 'The silk turns into a dagger. And the other thing – well, I'm not really sure, to be honest.'

Lily lifted her head. Puzzlingly, the look she was giving her was a mixture of amusement and confusion.

Sara frowned, but continued. 'I think I need to find the other two Hares for both of these things to work.' She stopped, even more puzzled. The amusement on Lily's face had gone. 'What…?' Sara asked, totally confused. Why wasn't Lily interested in the slice and the piece of silk?

Suddenly, Lily closed her hands, and Sara watched as the silvery slice and the piece of silk fell to the floor. The silvery slice bounced noisily a couple of times and ended up under her bed.

'Why did you do that?' Sara asked.

'Why did I do what?' Lily asked.

'Drop them.'

'Drop what?'

Sara stared at Lily. She had put the silvery slice and the piece of silk into Lily's hands and she had dropped them. 'I put them in your hands…'

Lily shook her head. She was gazing at Sara with what Sara now realised was something like pity. 'You didn't put anything in my…'

Sara dived under the bed. Pulling out the slice and still on her knees, she grabbed one of Lily's hands and forcibly opened its fingers. 'Feel it!' she cried, slapping the slice onto Lily's palm. 'It's real. It's a piece of metal with ragged edges and a picture of a hare on it! It makes a noise when it's dropped. Look at it! Just look!'

Lily pulled her hand away angrily. The slice fell again. 'You're scaring me!' she cried.

Sara, mouth open, gawped at her friend.

Lily stood up. 'I need to get going,' she said, grabbing her bag. She took two steps towards the door but stopped and turned around. 'Look, I think…' She paused. 'I think you're over-tired, maybe even exhausted. Will you try to get some sleep? We can talk again in the morning when you're feeling a bit better.'

Sara, still on her knees, glanced at the piece of silk. It had been kicked by Lily's shoe and was now lying crumpled in the corner of the room next to her wardrobe. For a moment, she considered barging past Lily, marching into the living room, and…

She sighed. No, the fact was she had failed. Lily wasn't joking. She really couldn't see – or even sense – the slice or the piece of silk.

It wouldn't do any good to show them to Mrs Ching. In fact, it would just make things worse. Perhaps the Immortals had expected her to do something like this. If they had, then well done! They had successfully thwarted her! Bravo! Good for them! What clever little Immortals they were! Sara clamped her jaws together, looked at Lily, and nodded.

'Promise?' Lily asked.

'Promise,' Sara replied quietly.

'See you,' Lily said.

'See you,' Sara replied, sure that Lily was still upset.

As soon as the bedroom door closed, Sara picked up the slice and the piece of silk. She wasn't crazy, but she was angry. She had been dragged into something that she hadn't asked to be part of, she had made a fool of herself, and she had upset Lily.

'I am *so* done with all of this,' she seethed and slammed the slice onto her computer desk so angrily, she accidentally hit the keyboard.

# CHAPTER 52

—

*MMMMMMMMMMZZZZZZZ!*

At first, she thought she had broken the keyboard and her laptop because its screen suddenly turned black and a high-pitched screaming noise filled the air. She reached down and pulled the plug, thinking her laptop was about to explode. When she straightened, she saw the screen had changed to white.

White?

As she watched, it flickered, flickered again, and a message box appeared in the top right-hand corner. Inside it, in black letters, was a title: *The Three Hares.*

Below the title, on the first line of a dialogue space, a cursor blinked. She sat down at her desk and nervously extending a finger, she touched the keyboard. No electric shock, no explosion – which was a relief!

The cursor continued to blink.

She began typing. At once, her words appeared next to a screen name that she hadn't chosen but which now made perfect sense.

---

**THE THREE HARES**
**First Hare**: Hello?

---

She waited.

And she waited.

And she waited.

It was a winter's evening when Sara noticed it. She had just returned from Granny Tang's apartment and had glanced at the screen before beginning her homework assignment.

The cursor was blinking. There were little dots…

Sara dropped the book she was holding, and, heart thumping, stared at the screen. She had been checking her computer for months: when she woke up, before she went to school, after she returned from school, before she went for a music lesson, before she went to bed. She had probably checked it hundreds and hundreds of times. And each time, through all those days and weeks and months, she had found the same thing: her hello remained unanswered in the top corner of the screen.

But now, after months of waiting, someone somewhere was writing a reply, and in a moment or two, that person's words would appear. Hunched over the screen, biting her lip, trying to breathe calmly, she waited for the words to appear.